Susannah gave Wyatt a smile.

"There's something comforting about watching children sleep," Susannah said. "They relax like there can't be anything wrong in the world."

"Then we lose that trust when we realize the world isn't always going to take care of us."

"Which you found out at an early age." Despair wavered in her voice. "I wish my children hadn't learned it so soon."

Wyatt closed his hands over her shoulders, massaging gently at the tense muscles under his fingers. "It'll be all right. You'll get through this. I'll make sure of it."

She sighed. "That feels good."

His body tightened at the husky tone of her words, but only a deep breath betrayed him. When she tilted her head to one side, he moved his grip to the cords between her shoulders and neck, still kneading at the stiffness.

"Wonderful," she whispered. After a few moments, she turned around to face him. In the dim light of the hall, she gazed up at him, her eyes wide and dark. "You're wonderful."

Dear Reader,

Families are wonderful. And complicated. They're built in different ways, through marriage and childbirth, but also through great friendship and mutual caring. Sometimes, everyone lives in the same little town—or the same big city—and they see each other nearly every day. Then again, some families are separated by long distances, even oceans or continents. Soon, I'll have one daughter and son-in-law living on the East Coast and one on the West Coast, with other members of the family spread out from Florida to Delaware. We get together only occasionally, but when we do, it feels as if we've never been apart. That's the best kind of closeness a family can know.

The Marshall Brothers books are all about family. Wyatt Marshall has held his together since he was sixteen, taking responsibility for his three younger brothers while his own hopes to be a husband and dad were dashed. As a teenager, Susannah Bradley ran away from her parents to start what she thought would be a terrific new life. Despite her two beloved children, though, her marriage has fallen apart. When Susannah takes refuge at Wyatt's ranch for the summer, these two wounded souls are drawn together, but taking a chance on new love is never as easy the second time around.

I hope you enjoy Wyatt and Susannah's story, the fourth book in the Marshall Brothers set. Please feel free to write to me—I love hearing from readers at my website, lynnettekentbooks.com, or via regular mail at PO Box 204, Vass, NC 28394.

Wishing you all the best and happy reading!

Lynnette Kent

A FAMILY IN WYOMING

—

LYNNETTE KENT

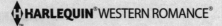
HARLEQUIN® WESTERN ROMANCE®

Recycling programs
for this product may
not exist in your area.

ISBN-13: 978-0-373-75736-7

A Family in Wyoming

Copyright © 2016 by Cheryl B. Bacon

Lynnette Kent lives on a farm in southeastern North Carolina with her six horses and six dogs. When she isn't busy riding, driving or feeding animals, she loves to tend her gardens and read and write books.

The Marshall Brothers owe their happy endings
to many of my friends and family...especially Abby,
who let me borrow a family story of her own,
as well as Sarah, Sandy, Pat and Lynna,
who took a sincere interest in these tales and
offered ideas, advice and lots of loving support;
Pam, who has ridden through most of my books
with me and is the specialist when it comes
to motivation and backstory; and, as always,
Martin, Elizabeth and Rebecca, who have
learned to live with my characters and talk
about them as if they were part of our family,
meanwhile putting up with a distracted and
occasionally desperate writer in residence.

To all of you, I offer my most heartfelt thanks!

I'd also like to say a word of appreciation
to Adrienne Macintosh, my editor for the
Marshall Brothers books, who has been
generous, patient, insightful and kind.

Working with you has been a
pleasure and a privilege.

Chapter One

June

Lying in wait at the screen door, Honey the golden retriever suddenly lifted her head. A moment later, Wyatt Marshall heard it, too—the rumble of a truck on the drive. With relief, he put down the book he'd been failing to read. "About time, isn't it, girl?"

Honey got up as he joined her at the door. Together they stepped outside just as headlights appeared in the distance. The six teenagers who'd been stationed on the front porch for the last two hours scrambled to their feet, cell phones forgotten for the moment.

"I was beginning to worry," Wyatt's youngest brother, Dylan, said as he came to stand beside him.

Garrett, the next oldest, posted himself at the foot of the steps. "I'm still worried. We don't know if they found Nate."

Wyatt shook his head. "Ford wouldn't come back without him."

The truck pulled to a stop in front of the house and Ford strode around the hood of the vehicle. "Sorry we took so long." He opened the front passenger door for Caroline Donnelly, the local social worker. "There were complications."

Wyatt frowned. "Is everybody alright?"

With her feet on the ground, Caroline offered a reassuring smile. "They will be, now that we've got them."

"*Them*?"

Ford opened the rear door and leaned inside. When he straightened up, he was cradling a young child in his arms. Then a woman emerged, followed by Nate Bradley. Nate was one of the camp kids the Marshalls were hosting on their ranch this summer. He'd run away earlier this evening—and gone straight home apparently.

Wyatt held the screen door as Ford led the way into the house and, without pausing, headed for the bedrooms down the hallway. Nate and the woman followed so quickly that Wyatt barely got a glimpse of her blond hair before they'd disappeared.

"His mother and little sister," Garrett explained, in response to Wyatt's questioning stare. "I guess finding Nate involved more conflict than we'd expected."

"We'd better make coffee," Wyatt said, and went to the kitchen. When Ford returned to the living room a couple of minutes later, Wyatt handed him a mug. "So what happened?"

After taking a long draw of the steaming brew, Ford sat down in a recliner by the fireplace. "Nate had gone home to check on his mom and sister. Unfortunately, his dad was in the house, drunk and furious. My arrival didn't improve the situation, and he started venting his anger on Nate. I lost my temper, too, but the deputy showed up and controlled the situation before any damage was done. Susannah—that's Nate's mother—didn't want to press charges, so we thought the safest plan was to bring her and her little girl, Amber, here." He drank more coffee. "I'll see about getting an order of protection in the morning."

In the silence that followed, a light step sounded in the hallway. Wyatt glanced up from his own cup as Susannah Bradley stepped into the room.

His gut clenched as if he'd been punched. Tall and shapely, with dark blue eyes and plump pink lips, she was a woman any man would want to look at twice. Or maybe always. Her bright blond hair was pulled away from her face, but soft strands fell free, begging to be brushed away, played with, twisted around a gentle finger.

What slayed him, though, were the bruises on her skin. A dark shadow along the line of her jaw, a purple-and-yellow stain under her right eye. A bracelet of red around her wrist.

Wyatt choked down the need to find the bastard who'd hurt her and extract payment. Instead, he got to his feet and nodded in her direction. "Welcome to the Circle M, Ms. Bradley. Have a seat." He motioned with his mug to the recliner by the fireplace and was relieved when she took him up on the offer. The light in the room shone indirectly there, calling less attention to her wounds. Though standing up aggravated the ache in his spine, sitting down felt worse, so he went to the entrance to the dining room and leaned a shoulder against the door frame.

"We made some hot chocolate for the kids," Garrett said. "Or there's coffee. Would you like a cup?"

Surprise tinged her smile. "You know, hot chocolate sounds wonderful. Thanks."

Caroline came through the front door. "I sent the other kids to bed." Her slender shoulders slumped and her face was pale. "It's been a long evening." She accepted her own cup of cocoa from Garrett and took a sip. "Mmm.

Just right." Then her gaze went to Susannah Bradley. "Did Amber settle in okay?"

"She fell asleep on the ride and never woke up. Nate's sitting with her in case she does, but I'm pretty sure she's down till morning." She pressed her lips together, glancing from Ford to Wyatt. "I can't ever thank you enough for taking us in. It's such a huge imposition, us just showing up in the middle of the night."

Wyatt put up a hand. "It's not a problem at all. I'm glad we're able to help. If there's anything else we can do, just say the word."

She turned her face away, blinking hard. He hated that he'd made her cry.

Once he'd finished his own cup of coffee, Dylan got up from the rocking chair. "Want me to walk Nate to the bunkhouse? I expect he's dead on his feet."

"Excellent idea." Ford stood, as well. "We all could probably use some sleep."

Caroline put a hand on Susannah Bradley's shoulder. "We'll get everything worked out. Just be confident that you and Nate and Amber are safe now."

"Thank you so much." She had a beautiful smile. And Wyatt could tell how it reassured her son when the boy followed Dylan into the room; Nate felt comfortable taking his own rest because his mom seemed to have everything under control.

But once Nate and the others stepped out the door, that smile disappeared. Bending her head, Susannah gazed into her mug, her brows drawn together and her lower lip between her teeth.

While Wyatt stood tongue-tied, Garrett sat down on the nearest end of the sofa. "Don't worry about the future," he told her. "You can let go tonight and face tomorrow's challenges after a good rest. All you have to do right now is relax." As a minister, he always knew what to say.

She drew a deep breath, but her shoulders remained stiff. "Travis is…unpredictable. If he followed us—"

This, Wyatt had the answer to. "You don't have to be concerned about him. If he does show up here, he won't get as far as the front steps."

Her gaze took in the brace he wore, and her eyes widened. "You're injured. And he might not make allowances…"

Garrett chuckled as he got to his feet. "Wyatt's pretty formidable, even with a broken back. And there are four of us, remember. There's nothing to be anxious about." He gestured toward the mug she cradled between her palms. "More?"

Susannah shook her head. "No, thank you."

"Well, then, I've got a couple of hours of work to put in on this week's sermon, so I'll say good-night now and see you in the morning." He nodded at Wyatt as he headed toward the back of the house. "Night, Boss."

"Night." They'd left him alone with Susannah Bradley. What was he supposed to do in this situation? His social skills, never all that adept to begin with, had rusted over the years through lack of use—he didn't spend much time socializing anymore. To cover his cluelessness, Wyatt went to take a gulp from his own cup, only to find it empty.

That gave him an idea. "We can put these in the dishwasher." He reached around the door frame and flipped on the dining room light. "It's this way."

Susannah followed as he skirted the table and chairs they used for most meals and pushed through the swinging door to the kitchen. When the light came on, he heard her gasp.

"What a beautiful room! I've never seen such a big kitchen!" As if she'd entered some kind of Wonderland, she wandered around, running a hand along the granite countertops, touching the cabinet doors, the drawer pulls, the edge of the stove. "How lovely it must be to cook here. So much space!" She faced him across the breakfast bar. "Did you build this house?"

He cleared his throat. "Not exactly. The bones were here, but we've done some renovating and additions over the years. Dylan's an artist, so the kitchen was basically his plan, with some help from a company in Sheridan." A question occurred to him. "Do you enjoy cooking?"

"Very much. You wouldn't believe it to look at him, but Nate loves to eat. I don't know how he stays so thin."

Wyatt opened the front of the dishwasher only far enough to ease the upper rack out part of the way. "Kids use up a lot of energy growing. I remember my brothers did."

Susannah came over to give him her cup. "He's certainly been growing—he's six inches taller this summer than last."

"Must be hard to keep him in jeans that fit. At least we had hand-me-downs." The front of the dishwasher rack was full. To pull it out all the way meant letting the door down, but that would require him to bend over to pick it up again—which hurt way more than he was ready to admit. They could just leave the cups in the sink and Garrett would take care of them in the morning...

"Let me," Susannah said. In one smooth move, she opened the door all the way, stowed the cups, and then shut the dishwasher.

Wyatt felt like a chump. "Thanks." Even to him, it resembled a growl.

But she didn't take offense. "You're welcome." She

leaned a hip against the counter and crossed her arms. "How did you get hurt?"

His face heated in embarrassment. "I was bucked off a young horse. He kicked up just as I threw my leg over, launching me like a rocket. I came down on my... I landed sitting down."

To his surprise, she chuckled. "I imagine that experience hurt your pride even worse than your back."

None of his brothers had dared to laugh at him. But her friendly gurgle was such a rich sound that he couldn't dredge up the least bit of dudgeon. Wyatt grinned. "Could be."

"Do you still have the horse?"

He nodded. "I'll break him next summer, when he's a year older and smarter. Sometimes they have to have more age on them."

"Meanwhile, you're going to spend this summer working with young humans, helping them become smarter."

"So we hope. As the local social worker, Caroline collaborated with Garrett to propose a summer camp for troubled kids on the Circle M and I liked the idea— though I'm not sure how much help I'll be, wearing this stupid brace."

He hadn't shared that hesitation with his brothers or Caroline when they'd discussed their plans. There was something about Susannah Bradley that turned him positively chatty. "I'm not used to spending my days in the house."

"I wouldn't expect so." She yawned suddenly and put up a hand to cover her mouth. "Sorry."

"No, it's late. And you've had a hard day. You should get some sleep. Anything you need?"

"Nothing at all." A soft blush colored her face. "I

don't know how I'll be able to repay your family for giving us refuge—"

Wyatt put up a hand and shook his head. "Don't even think about it. We're glad to help. Now go to bed. I'm the boss around here and that's an order."

"Yes, sir." Smiling, she crossed to the hallway door. "You're very kind," she said, before she left the kitchen.

Wyatt snorted to himself. Taking care of women and children didn't fall into the category of "kind," in his opinion. That was just a man's responsibility.

Susannah Bradley had obviously encountered a different type of behavior. Wyatt had never met her husband, but he'd heard talk about him around town. Travis Bradley had shown up about a year ago, asking for work at ranches in the area and bragging about his cowboying skills, his rodeo wins. Nobody who'd hired him kept him on for long because he eventually showed up drunk—or didn't show up at all.

Then Caroline Donnelly had proposed holding a summer camp for at-risk kids on the Circle M Ranch. Nate Bradley was one of those kids, a teenager who'd kept his secrets until tonight. Ford had encountered Nate's dad at a recent rodeo and then rejected the man when he came looking for a job on the Circle M. Thank goodness he had, since they'd now discovered just how bad Nate's home life could be when Travis took out his frustrations on his wife and kids.

But the Marshalls, with help from Caroline, would ensure that Travis never hurt his family again. As a lawyer, Ford would use his expertise to keep Bradley at a distance while Susannah figured out her next steps. Surely she had family she and her kids could count on for protection.

Realizing he was a long way from sleep himself,

Wyatt poured a new cup of coffee as he considered the situation. Since her family had clearly been of little help to Susannah so far, maybe they wouldn't take care of her and the kids the way they should now. In that case, she'd have to make her own way somehow, somewhere. But he couldn't believe she would choose to stay with the man who left those marks on her skin. No woman deserved that kind of abuse. If she didn't believe that fact, they would have to help her understand.

Returning to the living room, he eased himself into the rocking chair and picked up his book. Slumber didn't come easily to him these days, since lying down flat in bed hurt his back. So did sitting and standing, but at least he could occupy his mind while he was awake, instead of lying there useless in the dark.

Rather than reading, though, he found himself thinking about Susannah—with more attention to detail than was good for him. That silky hair, those plump lips… long, slender legs under a denim skirt…a straight spine, conveying pride and strength. Graceful, gentle hands, which could comfort a child.

Or pleasure a man.

This time he growled for real, low in his throat. The woman was married. Even if the marriage ended, she'd been treated badly by a man she ought to be able to trust. Why would she take such a risk ever again?

Besides, at the age of thirty-six, Wyatt considered himself a confirmed bachelor, not a prospect for happily-ever-after. Too set in his ways, too busy for romantic nonsense, too cranky to live with young kids. His brothers would testify to his contrary ways. They argued with him about it often enough.

So getting to know Susannah Bradley as anything besides a casual friend would not be wise. He would help her all he could and then send her and her kids on their way to a new, better life. That was the best he could do for them.

And the safest thing he could do for himself.

EARLIER THAT NIGHT, frantic and ashamed, Susannah had grabbed a nightgown while throwing together some clothes to bring away with her. But she hadn't realized it was this white one—the one with narrow straps, a low neckline and gossamer fabric that didn't leave much to the imagination. She'd found it in a thrift shop when they'd lived in South Dakota, about a year after Amber was born. Travis had kept the same job for six months and life seemed to be straightening out, finally. Maybe, she'd thought, they could make another baby. She would love to have more children.

Then the drinking got out of hand again, as it always did. He was fired from the job, couldn't find another, and so they moved on to Wyoming—Gillette, Sheridan, Buffalo, and now Bisons Creek, where their marriage and their life together had fallen to pieces.

Biting her lower lip, she folded up the nightgown and stuffed it to the bottom of her duffel bag, then eased down on top of the bedcovers still wearing her clothes. This serene bedroom, in shades of cream and coffee, was far and away the most luxurious place she'd stayed since leaving her parents' home. It was furnished with a queen-sized bed draped with a cozy comforter and softened by plenty of pillows, a dresser with a mirror above and two armchairs for relaxing, plus a private bathroom. The Marshall brothers offered their guests all the amenities she imagined could be found in an expensive hotel.

And her little girl had taken full advantage. Curled up on her side, a chubby thumb pressed into that pouty lower lip and blond curls tousled across the pillowcase, Amber slept deeply. She must be exhausted.

Her mother certainly was, but sleep had never seemed further away. Her brain wrestled endlessly with the mistakes of the past and the troubles of the present—not to mention the questions posed by an unknown future. Eyes burning, she yawned and shifted position but simply could not relax enough to doze off.

After two restless hours, she sighed and sat up, swinging her legs off the bed. Maybe a glass of water would help. Or a walk around the house. At this late hour, she wouldn't disturb anyone. She'd leave her shoes off to be sure she didn't make any noise on the wooden floors.

The long hallway was dark, all the doors except for the kitchen's closed. There, a light shone above the sink. She opened the upper cabinet to the right and found the drinking glasses just where she'd expect them to be. Smiling at having guessed correctly the first time, Susannah drank down two full tumblers of water and then set the glass in the dishwasher. She took a few minutes to appreciate the room yet again—she could picture racks of cookies and fragrant loaves of bread cooling on all this counter space. Amaretto cakes baked for Christmas, tomatoes and green beans and pickles canned in the summertime, a big Thanksgiving dinner with turkey and dressing and sweet potatoes and pies… This kitchen could produce all sorts of wonderful food for friends and family to enjoy.

She'd sorely missed friends and family since she and Travis got married. The only friends he ever made were his drinking buddies. His mother had disowned them both when she heard about their wedding. Her parents had been so hurt when she ran away, though they still called on her birthday…if they could find her. She and Travis had moved around a lot.

Remembering the home she'd left thirteen years ago, Susannah sighed and stepped toward the dining room. A kitchen like this was a dream she couldn't envision for herself. To be honest, she had no idea what she was supposed to do now. She didn't deserve anything special, but her children needed something better than they'd had. A safe, stable life. How would she manage that on her own? Where would they go?

Pushing through the dining room door, she was surprised to see a light on in the living room…and even more surprised to find Wyatt Marshall seated in the rocking chair.

She stopped short. "I'm sorry. I didn't think anyone would still be up."

He shook his head. "No problem. Can't sleep?" A big man, with broad shoulders and long legs, he seemed to dominate the spacious room. The big, golden dog lay at his feet, its tail thumping the floor.

Susannah swallowed against a sudden surge of nervousness. "Not yet."

"Sometimes your brain won't shut off even when you need it to." Thanks to the brace he wore, he was sitting bolt upright in the rocker, looking anything but comfortable. The strong planes of his face created an impression of austerity. But his deep-set brown eyes were compassionate. "Garrett is right. Worry and regrets won't change anything tonight. Right now your kids are safe. You've got friends you can count on. Your troubles will keep until morning."

"Until morning. Got it." Seeking a distraction, she nodded toward the book in his hand. "Is the story so good it's keeping you awake?"

A smile widened his well-shaped lips. "My back keeps me awake, but the book gives me something to focus on besides how much I'd rather be in bed." After a pause, he cleared his throat. "Asleep."

"What is the story about?"

With a finger marking his place, he showed her the cover, which featured a sword and a shield. "The Battle of Thermopylae in 480 BC."

Susannah frowned. "I don't know what that is. Was."

"A small force of Greek soldiers held off the Persian army for a week and then lost their lives defending a narrow pass through the hills. The soldiers' example inspired the rest of the country, and eventually the Persians were defeated in their attempt to take over all of Europe. It's a pretty important moment in history."

Examining the shelves flanking the fireplace, she saw that many of the volumes were about war. "Are battles your favorite subject?"

He came to join her in front of the books. "I enjoy history, especially military history. So much of human destiny has been decided on the battlefield."

She realized just how tall he was when she had to look up at his face. "I'm not sure that's a good thing."

His keen gaze met hers. "Facts are facts. If you aren't familiar with the past, you're just going to repeat it."

"Yes, I've heard that quote before. But maybe we use the past too often as a pattern, instead of searching for new solutions."

Wyatt closed his book and slotted it into an opening on the shelf, before turning toward her. "An interesting point of view. Sounds as if you've done some reading of your own."

"Not really. Not…lately." She moved away from the

shelves. Away from his attention. "My parents were both teachers. They talked about ideas at the supper table."

"That's a good way to learn."

Foolish, to bring up such painful memories. "It should have been. But I was a careless teenager, more involved with my friends and boys than what they had to say." Running a finger along the top of the rocking chair, she blew out a deep breath. "I wasted the opportunity."

"It's never too late to learn."

"Oh, I think sometimes it is. Right now I'm more concerned about what to do for Nathan and Amber than what happened thousands of years ago."

"You do have some decisions to make. Forgive me for butting in, but I'm hoping one of them isn't to go back to that bastard who hurts you."

The intense anger in his voice mirrored her own. "That's not an option. He stepped over the line tonight with Nathan. I can't let him hurt my children."

"Good for you."

She gripped the rail of the rocker with both hands. "But I don't know what comes next. Ford said something about an order of protection. Are we supposed to stay in the trailer after that? Where will Travis live? If he stays there, how will I get the children's clothes and toys?" Once again, concerns and uncertainties ambushed her, buzzing in from all directions. "Where will I get a job in a place as small as Bisons Creek? Or do we have to move to find work? Where? How can I secure a place to live without a paycheck? What about—"

Appalled, Susannah clapped her hands over her mouth to stop the flow of words. What had possessed her to unload on Wyatt Marshall like that? "I'm so sorry," she whispered from behind her palms.

He came to stand about an arm's length away. "I can solve a couple of those problems."

She uncovered her face. "You've already done more than enough. I shouldn't be bothering—"

"Maybe you ought to stay here for a while. At least for the summer, while your son's in camp."

"I couldn't possibly impose on you for so long."

"You could if you worked as our housekeeper and cook."

Hearing the words made her mind go blank. She could only stare at him in shock.

"Even if I wasn't trussed up in this brace, I've never been much good in the kitchen," he said with a lift of his big hands. "Or the rest of the house, for that matter. This summer, my brothers are going to be tied up with the ranch work I can't do, plus the kids in the camp. Dylan's got sculptures to work on, Garrett has his responsibilities at the church, and Ford will be going back to his law office in San Francisco soon. We really need somebody who can take care of this place, maybe put together a meal for me now and then. We would pay you, of course. And you'd be safe here while you got things... straightened out...with your husband."

"I—I don't know what to say." She could barely breathe, let alone think. "C-can I give you an answer tomorrow?"

"Sure. Whenever you decide. In the meantime, make yourself at home." His smothered yawn seemed too convenient to be real. "I believe I'm ready to hit the sack. Just flip the light off when you're ready." He stopped at the doorway to the hall but didn't glance back. "Night, Susannah. Come on, Honey."

She started, then realized that was the dog's name.

"Good night." On impulse, she added, "What time do you eat breakfast?"

Wyatt pivoted to face her again. He wore a big grin. "I'm sleeping late these days, don't get up much before six or six thirty." Touching two fingers to an invisible hat brim, he nodded. "See you in the morning."

Standing in the living room, Susannah listened as his footsteps receded down the hallway. Wyatt Marshall struck her as a remarkable man. Despite his injury, he seemed to be *in control*—of himself, of his surroundings, of life in general. And his generosity amazed her. Not only was he holding a summer camp for teenagers on his ranch, but he'd offered a solution to her most pressing problem—she and the children could stay on the ranch while she saved up the money she needed to find a new home and a real job. His kindness might even extend to giving her a reference she could use when she applied. How helpful that would be!

After turning out the living room lamp, she went back to the lovely guest room, where she saw that Amber still hadn't stirred. With her shoulders sagging under the weight of fatigue, Susannah folded down the covers on her side of the bed, finally ready to rest. She had just lifted her feet off the floor when her cell phone gave a familiar ring.

Travis.

She jumped up and grabbed her purse off the dresser, rummaged for the phone…but then hesitated as it rang again. Should she answer?

With the third ring, Amber frowned and her eyelashes fluttered. "Mommy?"

Susannah leaned over to put a palm on her daughter's shoulder. "Shh, baby. It's okay. I'm here." With her free hand, she pushed the button to talk. "Hello?"

"Susie? Susie, honey, where are you?" His words were slurred. "I miss you, sweetie. Come home." He'd moved through the anger phase of being drunk and would now become more and more maudlin. If she were there, she'd put him to bed and he'd sink into unconsciousness.

"Susie?"

"I can't come home." The words were hard to say. She'd loved him for so long. Just not anymore. "We won't be back, Travis."

"Don't say that. I'm sorry. I didn't mean it, honey." He sniffed hard, as if he was crying. "I'll change. Really, I will. I'll go to AA. That social worker can help me."

Thirteen years of promises were as much as she could take. "No, Travis. Not this time."

The rage flared up. "They're my kids, too. You can't keep them from me."

She squeezed her eyes shut and remembered Nathan, crumpled on the floor where his father had thrown him earlier that night. "I told you that if you hurt them, I would keep them away from you. And you did that tonight."

In the long silence that followed, she could hear his fractured breathing, could picture him trying to pull himself together.

"It doesn't have to be like this," he said. "Give me another chance, Susie. We'll make it work." When she didn't answer, he continued to plead. "We were good together, you know? We've had lots of fun, even with the kids. I can get it together, find a job. Don't give up on me, Susie, I swear—"

Susannah pressed the button to end the call and then turned off the phone altogether. As she curled up on the bed beside Amber, her eyes burned with tears. The despair she'd been fighting for hours threatened to swamp her.

She'd made such a mess of her life. Her children were suffering because of her foolishness, her bad choices. How could she ever compensate for those mistakes?

Wyatt's deep, warm voice came into her head. *Worry and regrets won't change anything tonight... You've got friends you can count on.* She recalled the concern in his brown eyes, the encouragement in his smile.

Friends. She hadn't had many of those over the years. Travis never liked the women she'd tried to connect with...or else he liked them too well. Susannah hadn't been blind to those affairs. But for some reason he had always come back to her.

Now, though, the Marshall brothers had declared themselves her friends. Caroline Donnelly would stand beside her, too. If they were willing to offer so much help, she couldn't let them down. Couldn't let her children down. Somehow she would have to dredge up the courage and determination to accept Wyatt's offer. She would spend the summer working for him, doing whatever she could to make his recovery easier, maybe help with the kids' camp, as well. Amber and Nathan would have a chance to recover from Travis's influence and experience a more settled, responsible way of living.

At the end of the summer, she would find a job, probably in a bigger town like Casper, or Cheyenne or Laramie. As for a divorce...she'd already filed the papers, which had only made the situation worse. Travis had never hurt one of the children until tonight, when he was notified of her petition. Now that he knew, he would put up every roadblock he could think of to keep the kids, including a custody battle, and the court might very well give him visitation, at least. Then he would be part of their lives forever. The prospect drenched her with dread. What would it take for them to be free?

With her thoughts still in turmoil, Susannah began to wonder if she'd be awake all night long. Sleep finally claimed her but only until the sound of a shower running somewhere in the house roused her at five thirty. Anxious to start her new job—her new life!—responsibly, she groped her way out of bed and into the bathroom, where a cold washcloth on her face and arms dispelled most of the brain fog. She donned a clean shirt and jeans, combed her hair and twisted it into a messy bun. She even managed to put on some lipstick. Just as the shower cut off, she left the guest room and made her way to the kitchen.

But the coffeepot defeated her. A stainless-steel monster with no obvious controls, it lurked on the counter, daring her to do something stupid and break it. The only coffee she found was a bag of whole beans, beside a grinder as intimidating as the brewer. Susannah hung her head. Not even six o'clock and she'd already failed.

"Well, good morning!"

She whirled to find Garrett Marshall standing in the doorway. His wet hair identified him as the one who'd taken the shower. "G-good morning. I was going to make some coffee, but…"

He sent her a grin nearly as appealing as his older brother's. "It's quite a contraption, isn't it? Dylan decided we should upgrade from the standard plastic-and-glass model." He joined her at the counter. "I will admit this version makes a great brew. Let me run you through the process."

Within minutes, they were sampling the results. Susannah savored the aroma rising from her mug. "I had no idea coffee could taste this rich. I'll have a pot made at about five thirty tomorrow. And breakfast at six thirty. Will that work for you?"

Garrett shook his head. "You don't have to worry about that. I usually make the coffee. As for breakfast—"

"It's my job," she told him with some pride. "Wyatt hired me last night to cook and keep house."

The man on the other side of the breakfast bar gazed at her for a long moment. Then he chuckled. "Of course he did. It's a great idea." He offered a handshake. "Welcome to the staff at the Circle M. Wyatt is the main one you'll be making breakfast for, besides yourself and Amber. Occasionally I'll need something, too, and maybe Dylan, those mornings after he stays up late working on his sculpture. The camp kids do most of their own cooking, so Ford, Caroline and I try to show up for their meals as a gesture of support. I expect to lose a good ten pounds this summer, when all is said and done."

She laughed with him. "I'll have a supply of cookies on hand, to keep your strength up."

"I'll hold you to that promise."

By six thirty, she'd explored all the cabinets and the refrigerator, started a pan of biscuits baking and arranged a place setting at the breakfast bar, where Garrett said Wyatt preferred to stand and eat. When she heard new steps coming down the hallway, she quickly poured a big cup of coffee and turned just in time to see Wyatt enter the kitchen. Wearing a wrinkled T-shirt and sweat pants, with his hair uncombed and his puffy-eyed face unshaven, he reminded her of a bear just coming out of hibernation.

She couldn't help smiling at him. "Good morning! Here's your coffee. How do you like your eggs?"

"Damnation," he growled, squeezing his eyes shut

for a few seconds. When he opened them again, he was scowling. "I'd forgotten you were here."

So much for the first day of her new life!

Chapter Two

July

"Will you play with me?" a little voice asked. "Please?"

Honey, dozing on the floor beside the desk, raised her head at the intrusion. Wyatt started to glance over his shoulder, but a stab of pain in his back stopped him. With an irritated snort, he swiveled his chair away from the computer instead.

But his bedroom seemed to be empty. "Who's there?"

The five-year-old peeked around the corner of his dresser. "Me." She eyed him nervously. "Amber."

Not wanting her to be afraid of him, he kept his tone gentle. "Why are you hiding, Me Amber?"

She glanced behind her. "My mommy said not to bother you," she said at a lower volume.

He smothered a smile. "So why did you?"

"'Cause I want to play Candyland." Coming out from behind the dresser, she displayed the game box she was holding. In a bright yellow T-shirt, green shorts and green sneakers, she reminded him of a cheerful dandelion. "And you can't play by yourself."

Wyatt remembered playing the game with Dylan when his brother was about this age. "Did you ask your mom to play with you?"

Her golden curls bounced as she nodded. "She has to dust the bookshelves. And wash the windows. And sweep the fireplace."

"That's a lot to do." In the short time she'd been there, Susannah Bradley had systematically overhauled the place, room by room. He scarcely saw her during the day, she stayed so busy. And the house had never been so clean, so easy to live in. The meals she prepared tempted him as food hadn't in years. On her breakfasts alone, he'd have been well fueled for a full day's work... if he wasn't stuck in the house with nothing to occupy him but wrangling numbers.

The least he could do was give her daughter a few minutes of his time. "Sure. I'll play with you. Come on in."

He rolled his chair over to the bed and they set up the board on the mattress, which Susannah made up for him in the mornings while he ate breakfast—an image he tried to avoid when he went to lie down at night. The image of her graceful hands smoothing his sheets did nothing to foster a good night's sleep.

"Now, this is how you play," Amber said, explaining the rules as she shuffled the cards with an endearing clumsiness. She was very serious about the process, frowning as she moved her piece from square to square, instructing him on the meaning of each card he drew. Even though he knew next to nothing about little girls, he felt he had the situation under control.

Until she landed on a licorice square. "No!" She bounced on the bed, upsetting the playing pieces and scattering the cards. "I don't want to lose my turn!"

He made the mistake of arguing. "That's the way you said the game works."

"But you'll get ahead of me," she wailed. "It's not fair!"

In the next moment, Susannah's voice came down the hallway. "Amber? Amber, where are you?" Then she stood at his door. "What in the world...?"

Getting to his feet, Wyatt cleared his throat. "We're... uh...playing Candyland."

Standing by the bed, she crossed her arms and glared at her daughter. "What did I tell you?"

Staring at her hands, Amber hunched her shoulders. "Not to bother him." Then she looked up. "But he wanted to play. Didn't you?" Wide blue eyes, still wet with tears, begged for his support.

"I did." He caught Susannah's gaze. "It's okay. Really. I've got nothing but time."

"You're very generous." Taking a deep breath, she let her arms relax. But a faint flush on her cheeks revealed that she was still upset. "You don't have to be a babysitter. It's not part of the arrangement."

"I'm not a babysitter," he shot back. Then he softened his tone. "I'm a friend. Amber's friend. And yours."

Her shoulders slumped slightly. "I know. I just...hate taking advantage. We owe you and your brothers so much already." Even though she must have been working hard, she seemed neat and fresh, her sleeveless blue shirt and khaki shorts as crisp as when he'd first seen her early this morning.

"You're helping us out." He put a hand on her shoulder. "And we're grateful."

She started under his touch. Her gaze flashed to his face and then away.

Wyatt withdrew his hand quickly, silently cursing himself. Like a mistreated horse, a woman who'd been abused would naturally be shy of men. How had he let himself forget?

"We're doing fine in here," he said then, jaw tense, fingers shoved into the pockets of his jeans. "Don't worry."

Stepping to the side of the bed, Susannah pointed a finger at her daughter. "No more tantrums over the game, Amber. You're a big girl and you know you have to play by the rules. Nathan taught you. Remember?"

"I 'member. I'll be good." She beamed an angelic smile. "Can we start over? I messed up the board."

Wyatt frowned at her. "I think I've been conned. But, yeah, we can start over."

He only wondered if he would have to do the same with her mother.

SUSANNAH WENT TO the kitchen and poured herself some coffee, cradling the mug with both hands to hold it steady.

Wyatt had touched her. And she'd jumped, like a nervous teenager. How stupid could she be?

She didn't believe for a second that he would hurt her. That wasn't the problem. But her own response had shocked her—an immediate urge to lean into his hand, to savor the warmth of his palm, the strength of his fingers.

Where had that come from?

The sound of footsteps heralded Caroline's arrival in the kitchen. "Good afternoon! I see you have a formidable project underway in the living room."

"I noticed the books needed dusting." Susannah gathered her scattered thoughts. "I'll have everything restored to order by dinnertime."

"I'm impressed that you decided to tackle it at all. There's no telling when—if ever—that chore was last attempted." Dark haired and petite, wearing jeans and a green T-shirt, boots and a white hat, she epitomized the perfect cowgirl. "I left Dylan and Garrett watching the kids jog their horses around the corral. I'm dying for some coffee to keep me awake." Pouring a cup, she sent Susannah a conspiratorial wink. "Too many late nights spent on the phone with Ford in San Francisco."

"When does he come back for good?" Though he'd meant to stay on the ranch for only a few weeks while Wyatt recuperated, falling in love with Caroline had inspired Ford to leave his law practice in California for his home and family in Wyoming. He'd brought with him the lovely engagement ring now resting on Caroline's left hand.

"At the end of the week, thank goodness. I can't believe how much I miss him."

Susannah realized she hadn't seen Travis for almost two weeks—and she hadn't missed him at all, had actually been more contented than she'd felt in years. Shame brought heat to her face. "I'm sure you do."

Caroline gazed at her for a moment and then crossed the kitchen to stand nearby. "You don't have to feel guilty," she said quietly. "He forfeited his claim to your concern, your love, the first time he hurt you. You and your children have every right to find a place where you're safe and cared for."

"I know." Susannah swallowed hard. "It's just...he wasn't always like...that."

"But you have to cope with the present, not the past."

"He could change." The possibility seared her conscience. "What if I gave up too soon?"

Leaning one hip against the counter, the cowgirl social worker ran a finger around the rim of her mug. "Do you think he will?" After a moment, she met Susannah's gaze. "Are you willing to risk Nate and Amber's well-being on that possibility?"

"No!"

Caroline nodded, lifting her mug in a salute. "You've made the smart and brave choice. Just take things one step at a time for a while. Let the past recede and the future wait awhile. For now, this summer, the three of you are in a good place."

Picturing the big man playing Candyland with her daughter, Susannah smiled. "You're right. We are."

Caroline stopped by the plate of peanut butter cookies on the kitchen table. "Mmm…these look delicious." She chose one and finished it off. "That Nate of yours is a natural horseman, by the way. He rides as if he's been in the saddle since he was a baby."

Susannah dumped the dregs of the coffee in the sink and poured out beans to start a fresh pot for Wyatt's afternoon consumption. "He's always loved horses. Whenever we went to the library, he found books about cowboys, ranches and riding. I'm sure he enjoys being here."

"I hope so. We'll see to it that he gets as much horse exposure as possible. Meanwhile, I'm taking one more of these cookies as I go. Once Dylan, Wyatt and Garrett find them, there won't be any left." She grabbed another cookie on her way out.

With the coffee made, Susannah decided she'd better check on the gamers in the room at the far end of the hall. Since Amber hadn't wandered off seeking new entertainment, Susannah expected to find them still absorbed in the colors of Candyland.

Her heartbeat quickened as she approached the doorway, which was ridiculous. Nothing had happened to make her nervous. She drew a deep breath and relaxed her clenched fingers. Maybe she'd indulged in too much coffee today.

When she stepped into the room, she was surprised

to find the game abandoned on the bed. Wyatt sat at his desk, with Amber on the floor beside his chair, her box of crayons and what seemed to be a ream of paper spread around her.

Amber glanced up as Susannah stood staring. "I'm drawing, Mommy." The page she held featured one diagonal blue line. "See?"

"That's…um…wonderful, honey." As far as she could tell, all the papers showed just one or two marks, on only one side. "You're making a lot of pictures, aren't you?"

Wyatt swiveled his chair around to face her. "She won two games," he said. When Susannah frowned in doubt, he held up a hand. "Fair and square. Then she wanted to use her crayons, so I gave her some paper." He glanced down at Amber, and his usually solemn expression softened into a smile. "She's having a good time."

"So I see." Flustered by his smile, Susannah hunkered down beside her daughter and gathered together the *drawings*. "You could put a picture on both sides, Amber. Can you do that?"

"Don't want to." Amber pulled open the bottom drawer of the desk and brought out more sheets. "I like it this way."

"I don't mind," Wyatt said. "As long as she's happy."

"She's making a mess and wasting supplies. And trees." Aware of how bitchy that sounded, Susannah stacked the pages and flipped them over, blank side up. "Draw on these, Amber. You don't want to use up all of Mr. Wyatt's paper."

Lower lip stuck out and eyes wide, Amber clutched the blank pages to her chest. "No."

Great. An argument, in front of Wyatt. Susannah kept her voice gentle. "You have plenty, sweetie. Leave the rest alone."

"I want more." In a quick move, she scattered the pages she was holding, turned to the open drawer and reached inside. "More!"

Face flaming, Susannah straightened up. "I'm sorry," she said, not meeting Wyatt's eyes. "You've been very good to play with her, but I think a break is in order." She picked up her wailing-and-kicking daughter by the waist. "I'll deal with this chaos in a few minutes."

"I can get—" he started, but stopped. "No, I can't," he said gruffly. "Damn this brace, anyway."

Having ruined a perfectly peaceful scene for her daughter and for him, Susannah took Amber to the room they shared and shut the door. A few minutes of sobs and sniffles followed, during a heart-to-heart talk about listening to Mommy, before her little girl fell asleep with the tears still drying on her face. Some days, a grown-up five-year-old still needed a nap.

Now she had to go back and face Wyatt while she restored order to his office. He kept his life organized, she'd discovered since she'd been here. Much of her cleaning had been out of a sense of duty more than actual necessity because the house was amazingly tidy, especially considering bachelors lived there. Despite what he'd said, having the floor carpeted with child-ish scribblings had probably driven him crazy. Susannah knew she shouldn't have allowed her daughter to demand so much of his time. She'd make sure she kept closer tabs on Amber in the future.

In the next few days, that resolution proved much easier to make than to keep. Whenever Amber's bright voice had gone quiet, Susannah would discover her playing with Wyatt. She found them in the living room one afternoon, where Wyatt sat in the rocking chair with the baby doll, wrapped in a bath towel, resting on his shoulder. Amber stood beside him, patting the baby's shoulder as he moved back and forth.

"What are you doing?" had become her standard question.

"Shh!" Amber put a finger to her lips. "Baby is sick. Her daddy is rocking her to make her feel better."

"Ah." She kept her voice down. "And who are you?"

"I'm the sister. He's my daddy, too."

Struck to the heart, Susannah found her gaze locked with Wyatt's, but she couldn't read his expression. In desperation, she put a hand on Amber's shoulder.

"Sweetie, maybe the baby wants a drink of water. Why don't you go get her bottle from the bedroom?"

"Okay."

"I'm sorry," Susannah said as soon as Amber was gone. "I can't imagine where she comes up with these ideas."

"I expect you hold her when she's sick and that comforts her." The doll still rested on his shoulder. "Good parents do those things for their kids. And you're a very good parent."

"But I'm sorry you're getting caught up in her silly games. Really, you don't have to—"

"Susannah." His firm tone halted the frenzy of her speech. "You've said 'I'm sorry' twice in the last two minutes. Seems we never have a conversation lately without you saying 'I'm sorry.'"

She opened her mouth but couldn't think of anything that wasn't an apology, so she closed it again.

"Don't worry so much. Not about me." He glanced down at the doll and smiled. "I enjoy playing with Amber, seeing how a little girl's mind works. I'm not doing anything I don't want to do."

"If you're sure…"

"I'm sure you can stop apologizing. You and your kids are not a burden and you're not intruding. Just make yourself at home. Settle in. Or else I'm going to get mad." He sent her a wink. "You wouldn't like me when I'm mad."

EVEN AS THE words left his mouth, Wyatt realized his mistake.

"I'm so sorry." His turn to apologize. "That was a stupid thing to say. It's a joke between my brothers and me—from an old TV show."

To his great surprise, she laughed. "I know. I watched *The Incredible Hulk* reruns when I was a kid. I loved how he grew all big and green and furious."

Despite her good humor, his guilt persisted. "I didn't intend to threaten you." He considered the phrase again. "Although that's exactly the way it sounded."

"You were teasing, Wyatt. I got that." Her smile faded. "Travis doesn't threaten. He just…explodes."

"I hate reminding you of him." And hated remembering his own dad's hair-trigger temper.

"It's not as if I ever really forget." She drew a deep breath and then made an obvious effort to improve the mood. "You seem pretty experienced at holding babies. Did you spend a lot of time taking care of your younger brothers?"

"My mom was sick for a while before she passed away, so I did a fair amount of babysitting. Especially with Dylan."

"No wonder you're so good with Amber! Though after taking care of three younger brothers, I would expect you'd had enough of dealing with children. Yet here you are sponsoring a summer camp."

"Kids are important." He'd planned on having a full

house, back in his twenties when he'd believed getting married was part of his future. Too bad for him, the girl he'd loved wanted a different kind of life. Now everything he did was for the ranch and his brothers. "Caroline and Garrett proposed having the Circle M host the teenagers, and I decided we owed it to Henry to help the kids the way he helped us." And that was as close as he'd ever come to that long-ago dream.

Susannah gave him a puzzled frown. "Henry?"

"While I was growing up, we lived in town, where my dad repaired cars at the service station. After he died, I went to work out here for Henry MacPherson. Eventually he had all of us move in with him. And he left the four of us the ranch in his will."

"You lost both parents?" Her blue eyes widened. "That's so sad. How old—" She broke off the question as Amber returned to the living room. "Did you find the bottle, sweetie? That's good. Sick babies need to drink."

Now feeling a little foolish, Wyatt shifted the doll to the crook of his arm. "Maybe you should rock the baby for a while, Amber. I think that might help her get well." With a push on the chair arm, he got awkwardly to his feet.

"It's a him," Amber said, clambering into the rocker. "Russell." With a serious, concerned expression, she cradled the doll against her body and offered him the bottle.

"I could use something to drink, myself," Wyatt said, keeping his voice low. "Coffee, maybe?"

"I've just made a fresh pot." Susannah led the way through the dining room. "Russell was her friend when we lived in Gillette," she said. "His family had the house next door and the two of them would play together most of the day. That was two years ago, but she still asks about him sometimes."

"Changes are hard on kids." Wyatt reached above her head to push open the kitchen door.

"You would know. And I'm afraid, since we've moved so often…" she said, walking past him. "But now—" She stopped short, just inside the doorway. "Well, hello, Dylan!"

His brother's voice came from the kitchen. "Afternoon, Ms. Susannah. How's your day going?"

Following, Wyatt didn't stop as quickly, so he bumped into her, knocking her off balance. He put his hands on her narrow waist to steady her. "Sorry about that. You okay?" The world seemed to halt for a moment as he held her. Under his palms, she drew a deep breath and blew it out again.

"Of course. I'm fine." She stepped out of his hold. "Dylan, what are you doing hanging around the kitchen in the middle of the afternoon?"

Dylan saluted Wyatt with a lift of his coffee cup. Then he refocused his attention on Susannah. "Actually, I'm on a mission—I was sent to find cookies. Garrett said you were baking this morning and the kids were hoping…"

Arms crossed, she eyed him skeptically. "The kids?"

He winked at her. "Of course. Pure altruism on my part."

"I'm sure." She nodded toward a plastic container on the counter. "Those are the cookies. All ready for *the kids*." Her emphasis on the last two words drew Dylan's grin.

"I'm sure *they* will appreciate the effort, and I'll say thanks in their place."

Susannah smiled at him. "They're welcome."

Still standing by the kitchen door, Wyatt felt very much outside the conversation, as if he wasn't in the room at all. Dylan had always been a ladies' man, able to win a smile from females nine years old to ninety. That had never bothered him before. Wyatt wasn't sure why he resented his brother's easy charm this afternoon.

"I had a couple of other things to talk over with you, if you've got a minute," Dylan was saying.

"Sure." Susannah leaned a hip against the counter. "What's going on?"

Wyatt remembered he'd come in for coffee. Jaw set, he stalked across the kitchen and elbowed his brother away from the machine so he could pour a cup.

Prodded into motion, Dylan joined Susannah by the breakfast bar. "First off, that reporter is gonna show up here tomorrow to interview me. So if you could freshen up the other guest room, that would be great."

"No problem," she told him. "But I've been wondering, how did this house end up with two guest rooms?"

Wyatt started to answer, but Dylan spoke first. "You and Amber are staying in what used to be my room before I moved into the loft in my studio. Comfortable, isn't it?"

"Incredibly comfortable. We appreciate you sharing with us."

"Anytime." His grin could only be called flirtatious. "Meanwhile, we grown-up types were talking about giving the kids a picnic on Thursday, down at the creek, on the other side of the barn."

"Where the picnic tables are? That sounds like fun. I've walked there with Amber. She wants to play in the water."

"I imagine they all will. We also thought we'd give them a day off from making their own meals and put you in charge of the food, if you don't mind. Sandwiches, fruit, that kind of thing. More cookies would be good." Another of those grins.

And Susannah smiled in response. "I don't mind at all. I'm glad to help with the camp in any way I can. You'll want everything ready by noon?"

"Sounds about right. We'll show up and let the kids carry everything down to the creek. There are a couple of picnic baskets around here somewhere, I believe. And I'm sure we've got at least one big water cooler, plus an ice chest or two. Wyatt probably knows where they are. Right, Boss?"

Wyatt cleared his throat. "I do, yes." He couldn't believe he sounded so pitiful. "That kind of stuff is stored in the attic. I can bring it all down."

Dylan frowned at him. "I'm pretty sure climbing ladders is on the list of things you're not supposed to do for the next few months, along with riding horses. I'll fetch what we need. In fact, I'll do that right now." He set down his mug. "Come on, Susannah. Let's get this project underway."

Wyatt stayed where he was, fuming at…well, at the situation, more than anything else. At himself, for getting hurt. At being stuck in the house like an old man. Maybe he wasn't a kid anymore, but he could hold his own against any of his brothers when it came to ranch chores.

And, yeah, he was ticked off at his youngest brother, though he wasn't sure why. Dylan was just being himself—easygoing and sociable. His beguiling approach with women had never bothered Wyatt in the past.

Susannah, though… Susannah deserved to be treated with respect and deference. Not that Dylan had been disrespectful, exactly, but sometimes women took his flirting more seriously than he intended. As she recovered from a miserable marriage, she didn't have to be confused by casual gallantry. Should he say something to Dylan?

Should he warn Susannah?

He couldn't bring himself to speak to either of them, but in the days following he kept an eye on them when they were together, trying to judge how things were going.

But then the reporter from New York arrived, and Dylan immediately fell head over heels in love with her. Susannah didn't seem bothered by that obvious fact. When everyone sat on the front porch in the evening to enjoy hand-cranked ice cream, or when they gathered in the living room for a sing-along by the fireplace, Wyatt couldn't detect any difference between the way she behaved with Dylan and with Garrett or Ford. Or himself.

Which was as it should be. The only way it could be, for Susannah's sake.

ONCE SHE'D CLEANED every other space in the house, Susannah had no choice but to tackle Wyatt's bedroom. Just proposing the idea to him made her palms damp and her throat tight.

"I wondered—" she started one night during supper, while Amber was busy with her favorite meal of noodles topped by marinara sauce. "I wondered if I could spend some time in your room tomorrow."

Wyatt looked up from his lasagna, a startled expression on his face.

"Cleaning, I mean. I've done Ford's room and Garrett's. It's…um…your turn."

"Oh." He nodded. "Well, sure. That'll be great. I can work somewhere else while you're in there."

"I'll start with your desk area and try to finish as fast as I can. I don't want to interrupt you."

"These days, with the bad news I'm getting over the internet, being interrupted isn't such a problem." He was toying with his food, forking through it but not eating much.

Susannah rested her folded arms on the table. "What kind of bad news?"

"Prices, for one thing. Grass-fed beef, the kind we raise, is more expensive than conventional feedlot meat. A good portion of our market is the restaurant industry, but they're rejecting the higher prices and serving other proteins, like pork and chicken. So demand for the product is down, meaning lower prices. But the cost of living—not to mention the cost of producing these cattle—doesn't go down."

"I'm not much help with economics," she said. "But for what it's worth, yours is the tenderest, most flavorful meat I've ever cooked with."

Wyatt let out a big laugh. "That's the best thing you could have said. Maybe what we need is an advertising program to appeal to the public. You can star in the TV commercials."

Susannah felt herself blushing. "Not very likely."

"Why not? You're certainly pretty enough."

She stared at him, her breath caught in her chest. Wyatt's expression said he'd surprised himself.

"You *are* pretty, Mommy." Amber chose that moment to join the conversation. "I want to watch you on TV."

Thankful for the intrusion, Susannah turned to her daughter. "And I want to watch you finish up your green beans. Can you do that?"

Amber heaved a put-upon sigh. "Okay."

Wyatt didn't so much as glance up from his plate for the rest of the meal.

He was still avoiding her gaze when she saw him at breakfast the next morning. "I'll get started on your room right away," she said, hoping for interaction of some kind. "And work as fast as I can."

"Dylan plugged in my laptop in the dining room." Buttering his biscuit seemed to require all his attention. "And Amber is going to bring her coloring in to keep me company." Despite himself, he flashed a quick smile in her direction. "We'll be fine."

As soon as the kitchen was set to rights, she started in Wyatt's room. With some hesitation, she approached the big desk, where a computer screen and keyboard, along with multiple stacks of papers, books and magazines, obscured most of the space. In order to thoroughly dust the top, she would have to move them all. Did they have to be returned to exactly the same spots? How would she remember what went where?

She'd just moved the first pile to its corresponding position on the bed when Wyatt's footsteps sounded in the hall. "I need a couple of reports," he said as he entered the room. Then he stopped, hands on his narrow hips, surveying her and the desk. "You have to move all my stuff?"

Susannah decided to take the firm approach. "Yes," she said simply and then relented at his worried frown. "I'll replace them exactly the same way. I promise."

He blew out a short breath. "I'll do it." Stepping to the desk, he reached for a stack of magazines about a foot high.

Having him in the room while she worked would be... distracting. But she couldn't just shoo him away. "Those will be heavy. You shouldn't—"

Without a word, he lifted the pile and, following her lead, set it down on the mattress. They worked together in silence for a few minutes, moving back and forth past each other, sometimes brushing shoulders, until Susannah's nerves got the better of her.

"I didn't realize ranching involved so much paperwork," she volunteered in desperation.

"Most of it is done on the computer now. But I often refer to Henry MacPherson's record books. They cover more than four decades." Wyatt moved another set of papers. "I started out on paper, because he was teaching me. About five years ago I switched to the computer." He surveyed the contents of the bed. "Doesn't look like it, I guess. I'm still transferring relevant information from paper to digital."

"What kind of information?" Conversation made him seem less overwhelming. "What do ranchers keep track of?"

"Everything to do with the cattle—breeding, birthing, weaning, vaccinations, weigh-ins, culling, castrating, branding, health records, sales and purchases. Files on the machinery and vehicles we use, plus purchase forms and maintenance. Tax documents and all the receipts to go with them." He slid the keyboard and screen for the computer on the desk out of her way, so she could dust underneath. "And then there are deeds and notices for the grazing land we lease from the government. A couple of those piles of paper are from the Bureau of Land Management—and that's from just this year."

"Amazing." Moving between the desk and the wall, she cleaned the window frame and sill, and then she started on the panes. "You said Mr. MacPherson taught you, but you must have the education to manage such a complicated business. Not to mention knowing how to use the computer software. Did you get a business degree?"

Behind her, Wyatt chuckled. "Not hardly."

Susannah looked at him over her shoulder. "What do you mean?"

"I quit school when I was sixteen to go to work. I've been a cowboy ever since."

She pivoted to face him. "I didn't realize. You were that young when your dad died?"

He nodded. "Dylan was eight."

"The four of you grew up without your parents. And you've learned to manage all this—" she said with a gesture at the view of the rolling pastures framed by the window "—on your own."

"Henry taught me pretty much everything I know."

"Is this what you always wanted to do? Did you dream of being a cowboy as a little boy?"

His gaze seemed to turn inward. "Not that I remember. We played soldiers, or ball games, I think." He shrugged. "But ranch work was available when I needed a job, so that's what I did."

"Still…" The scope of his responsibilities amazed her. "You raised your brothers by yourself. From such a young age."

"We raised each other. That's why we stick together."

Some men were just born to be responsible. And some men weren't—like her husband.

Coming out from behind the desk, she didn't realize she'd revealed her state of mind until Wyatt said, "What's brought that frown to your face?"

"Oh." Her turn to confess. "Thinking about Travis, of course. His parenting skills—or lack of them."

"A good reason to keep him out of your life as much as possible."

"That's not—"

A sudden clatter sounded in the front of the house, followed by Amber's voice. "Uh oh."

Susannah rushed down the hallway and into the dining room. "What happened?"

Amber stood by the wall, a coloring book dangling from her hand. At her feet lay a laptop computer.

Wyatt's laptop computer.

"I tried to go over it," she said, pointing to the cord, which was plugged into the wall. "But my foot caught it." Judging from her big eyes and frightened expression, she understood the seriousness of the problem.

Wyatt joined them. "I can't get down there with this stupid brace on," he said in a quiet voice. "Could you set it on the table?"

Susannah bent to pick up the computer. As she straightened, she glanced at the machine and gasped. The screen was cracked and crazed, the image totally destroyed.

A long, low whistle escaped Wyatt's lips. "That doesn't look good." She put it on the table and he pressed some keys, typed a string of letters. The screen went dead. "Not good at all."

Chapter Three

Wyatt looked up from the busted computer to find Susannah and Amber staring at him with nearly identical expressions on their faces. There was dread, even fear in their eyes.

They expected him to explode, like Travis Bradley would. Like his father had, that last night, before stomping out of the house in a drunken rage.

Their reaction cut him to the bone. For a few seconds, he couldn't find the words to respond. He was not his father.

"I sorry," Amber said in a tiny voice, her tone a plea. "Can you fix it?"

He pulled in a deep breath. "Maybe. I'll take it to the computer shop in Casper, see what they can do." Then he met the little girl's gaze. "It was an accident," he said as gently as he could. "They happen. It's okay."

"Use my wages to buy a new one." Susannah put a hand on Amber's shoulder. "I insist."

"That won't happen. Really. It's okay."

"You're kind to say so." Her frown eased slightly. "But it's not, really."

"We're not going to argue over this." He blew out a frustrated breath. "I think I'll spend some time in the barn, watch the kids ride. And I'll eat lunch with them in the bunkhouse."

"Wyatt—"

"If you'll unplug the cord—" He hated having to ask. "Thanks." With the cover closed and the cord coiled on top, he pushed the laptop to the center of the table. "You two have a good afternoon."

Walking up the hill to the barn, he acknowledged the anger simmering in his chest. Anger at Travis Bradley, for conditioning his family to expect violence when they made a mistake. How could such a man live with himself?

He also had to admit to being angry that Susannah would put him in the same category as Bradley, if only by reflex. Wyatt had done his best, since she'd been here, to be reassuring, to appear totally safe. He *was* safe, dammit. Why would she think otherwise?

A single step into the shadows of the barn brought the sweet aroma of hay to his nose. Almost immediately, his temper started to cool. Walking along the side aisle, breathing deeply, he let the peace of the place soothe him. He'd spent too much time in the house this last month. Of course he was irritable.

At the back of the barn, he wanted to prop his arms on the half door leading out to the corral, but the brace restrained him from bowing his shoulders. So he stood stiff as a stick, instead, watching the teenagers ride their horses. With Dylan leading the line on his Appaloosa, Leo, the kids rode patterns around the ring—circles, diagonals, even serpentines. And they were jogging, which constituted great progress since Wyatt had last observed them.

He couldn't help noticing that Nate, Susannah's son, seemed more comfortable with his horse's motion than any of the riders except Dylan. He sat easily in the saddle, arms relaxed and steady, not flapping up and down in imitation of bird wings. His long legs were wrapped around the mare's barrel and stayed still in the stirrups. Caroline and his brothers had mentioned the boy's natural ability. Now Wyatt witnessed it for himself—they had a prospective cowboy on their hands.

The rest of the kids deserved encouragement, too, and he tried to speak with each one as they came in the barn to put away saddles, bridles and blankets.

"Good job," he said, as Thomas Gray Cloud lugged his saddle into the tack room. "You're keeping your hands down really well at the jog."

The boy fiddled with the way the stirrup was hanging. "Sometimes." He shrugged and, with a quick glance at Wyatt, headed for the door.

Only to run straight into Marcos Oxendine.

"Hey, watch it," Marcos shouted. "You about knocked me down."

Thomas glared at him. "Like you don't weigh twice as much as me. Give me a break."

"I'll give you a break. I'll break every—"

"That's enough." Wyatt used his own version of loud. "There's no call for an argument. Just stand back, Thomas, and let him get inside with his gear."

Rolling his eyes, Thomas moved out of the way until the other boy had come through. But when he tried to leave, Lizzie Hanson blocked his way.

"Oh…hi, Lizzie. I'll move." He retreated again. That was an interesting development—Thomas being nice to one of the girls.

"Thanks, Thomas." Blonde and boy-crazy, Lizzie fluttered her mascaraed lashes. "Can you put my saddle away? That would be so great." Then she noticed Wyatt's raised eyebrow. "Okay, never mind. I'll do it." One of the camp rules was that each rider was responsible for their own tack.

"You're looking comfortable in that saddle," Wyatt told her. "You and Major seem to be getting along well."

She gave him a wide smile. "I love him." Lizzie had been afraid of horses at the beginning of the camp, but Major, a brown, white and black pony, had proved to be just the partner she needed.

Nate was the last of the teens to leave the corral because he spent the longest time brushing his mare, Blue Lady. Thin and quiet, he kept his gaze down as Wyatt spoke to him.

"You're a born horseman, Nate. I appreciate the way you take care of your animal."

"Thanks." He glanced up briefly. "I want her to be clean. Comfortable."

"A real cowboy does exactly that." Wyatt's turn to hesitate. "So…you're having a good time? Enjoying the camp?"

"Sure. It's fun." He straightened his shoulders and, finally, looked Wyatt squarely in the eye. "Thanks for taking care of my mom and my sister. I was worried about them."

"We're glad to help. We'll make sure all of you stay safe."

Nate took a deep breath. "I hope so." He didn't sound convinced.

Before Wyatt could reassure him, Dylan looked in the door. "There you are, Nate. We were counting heads and missing one. Lunch is almost ready."

"Right." With obvious relief, Nate slipped out the door.

"Good to find you in the barn, Boss." Dylan waited

as Wyatt closed the tack room door behind him. "I think the kids are doing really well."

"That's what I saw." They walked toward the front of the barn together. "I'm not so sure about you, though. You seem kind of peaked."

After a brief, intense affair, Dylan's reporter had returned to New York. Working harder than ever on his sculpture, with occasional breaks to help out with the camp or ranch chores, the youngest Marshall was obviously suffering.

"I'll live," he said with a shrug. "I don't intend to die of a broken heart, if that's what you're worried about."

They stepped out into the bright afternoon and headed toward the bunkhouse where the kids ate their meals. "I wouldn't expect you to. But the process of healing can be painful." His own experience with first love had demonstrated the intense ache of rejection.

Dylan was silent for a minute. "Do you ever think about her? Marley Jennings? You still hear her name on the rodeo news these days, winning barrel races across the country."

"It's been more than ten years since we were together."

"Yeah, I know." Dylan gave a hollow laugh. "I'm just wondering how long I should expect to feel this way."

Wyatt clapped a hand on his shoulder. "Not forever. You'd be surprised how soon the memories fade." If he put his mind to it, though, he could recall the sight of her riding into an arena, her long, jet-black hair catching blue sparks from the floodlights, her palomino horse prancing as they carried the American flag along the rail. The epitome of a rodeo queen.

And not in the least interested in becoming a rancher's wife.

"A woman has a right to the life she wants," he said, aware the words wouldn't comfort his brother. "You can't expect them to give up their ambitions and dreams just because you fell in love."

"Yeah. I figured that out." Dylan opened the door to the bunkhouse. "Isn't it just great, being *enlightened*?"

Wyatt remembered the fear on Susannah's face.

Not today, he thought and followed his brother inside.

THE TEASING BECKY RUSH had been expecting started during lunch.

"Hey, Becky." Marcos sat down across the table from her. "Nice tan."

"Thanks." Feeling her sunburned face get even hotter, Becky tried to play it cool. "I thought I'd try a new look." She'd overslept this morning and, in her hurry, had forgotten to put on sunscreen. Then she'd left her hat in the cabin and hadn't had a chance to get it before their trail ride. Now, thanks to the bright summer day, her face was almost the same color as her red hair. Her arms, up to the sleeves of her T-shirt, matched perfectly.

From the chair next to Marcos, Thomas pointed at her with his knife. "What look is that? The lobster?"

Becky sent him a sour smile. "Ha ha."

Sitting on her right, Lizzie giggled. When Becky glared at her—they were supposed to be best friends—the other girl shrugged. "It was a funny thing to say."

Marcos pretended to be concerned. "Now, at least, you can hardly see the freckles."

That one hurt. She hated her freckles, the only thing she'd gotten from the dad who'd walked out on them.

The next comment came from Becky's left. "Leave her alone," Nate said. "You don't want anybody making fun of your color, do you?"

Marcos immediately got mad. "What's there to make fun of? Huh?"

"Nothing. Which is my point."

The other boy looked confused. Thomas cracked a laugh. "He told you, man."

Nate stared at him. "You, too."

Pushing quickly to his feet, Thomas propped his fists on the table and leaned across, toward Nate. "Listen here—"

Becky caught her breath, and her chest tightened in a way she was all too familiar with. She hated arguments. Thomas and Marcos had been in trouble more than once this summer for fighting each other. Even though there were grown-ups in the room, she didn't doubt for a minute that either one of the other boys could and would take Nate down. He was tall but thin, not at all a match for the stronger guys.

But he stayed sitting, as calm and controlled as usual in the face of the Thomas's anger.

Like wind blowing against the face of a high cliff, that fury ended up with nowhere to go. "Stupid," Thomas muttered, sitting down and picking up his sandwich. "Just stupid." He and Marcos both made a point of attacking their food, not talking to anyone, even each other. In record time, they'd finished, dumped their plates by the sink and left the bunkhouse. In another minute, Lizzie threw her half-finished food in the trash and followed them out. As usual, Lena and Justino sat together at the end of the table in their own little world— they probably hadn't even noticed what was going on with everybody else.

Left pretty much alone with Nate, Becky tried to forget how silly she must look with her face the color of a tomato. "Thanks," she said quietly. "I appreciate the defense."

He shrugged one shoulder. "I know what it's like to be bullied by those two. They shouldn't get away with it."

"You were so quiet, though. At my house, people— my mom and grandma—yell when they argue. Which they do most of the time." When they weren't too drunk or stoned to talk at all. She didn't want to admit that part.

"My dad yells." He started to say something else and then stopped.

But Becky had noticed the bruise on his jaw the morning in June after Mr. Ford had brought him back to the ranch. She could guess what else his dad did. "I hole up in my room a lot," she confessed. "Out of the way…if I'm lucky."

Nate's fingers were busy, crumbling the half of his sandwich he hadn't eaten. "Sometimes luck isn't enough."

"No." Funny that they were sharing this personal stuff when they didn't really know each other that well. They were in the same grade at school but went to different classes—Nate was one of the smart kids in the more advanced courses while Becky only did what she had to to pass at the regular level. What would be the point? Nobody in her family had ever gone past high school. She didn't expect to be the first.

"I guess we've got rodeo practice this afternoon," he said, breaking into her thoughts. "Are you going to compete?" They'd watched a couple of rodeos since they'd been at camp, but Mr. Garrett had announced that morning at breakfast that there would be a junior rodeo up in Buffalo at the end of August and anyone who wanted to could enter an event. Thomas, Marcos and Lena were all excited about the possibility of riding bulls, and they'd been practicing on a bucking barrel for weeks now.

Becky and Lizzie had been learning how to do barrel racing with Ms. Caroline—a timed event which involved running a cloverleaf pattern on their horses. "I'm not sure. My horse, Desi, and me, we're not too fast—mostly still trotting. I'm not sure I'll be ready. What about you?"

Getting to his feet, Nate shook his head. "Probably not. I like just riding around, without risking my neck." Picking up his dishes, he nodded in her direction. "See you at the barn."

"Sure." She watched him walk away, noticing his straight back and long legs, the soft brown color of his messy hair. Why hadn't she noticed before how cute he was? Cute guys who stuck up for girls with freckles and red hair were hard to find. Even harder to get to know.

But she and Nate had more than a month of camp left—plenty of time to become friends. More than friends. Unlike Lizzie, she'd never had a boyfriend, but now she thought it might be nice to have a boy around who understood her, who would fight for her.

Here at the ranch, where they saw each other every day, getting him to notice her, to like her, would be easier than in the crowded bustle of school. And she wouldn't have to bring him home if they wanted time together. She never brought anybody home.

Cleaning up after lunch with Justino and Lena, Becky found herself smiling for no real reason, except that today was a good day. Sure, her face and arms burned as if she had a fever. But because of that, she'd decided to have her first boyfriend.

And she wouldn't let the freckles stand in her way.

FOR THE FIRST time since she'd arrived at the Marshall brothers' home, Susannah was uncomfortable. And it was her own fault.

Wyatt hadn't said anything, of course. She would have been relieved if he had—then she could apologize, assure him she wasn't afraid, had never believed he would hurt her or Amber. Her reaction over the broken computer had been involuntary. Unthinking. Stupid.

The weekend passed and the opportunity she wanted never seemed to present itself. When she did see him—at breakfast—Wyatt was polite but quiet and aloof. He spent more time out of the house than he had since she'd come to stay, ate more meals with the teenagers in the bunkhouse. Short of following him around the ranch, how would she get a chance to talk to him?

Then, on Monday morning, disaster struck. Lena Smith collapsed and was sent to the hospital. Fortunately, the town's new doctor, Rachel Vale, had arrived and was able to support Garrett as he managed the situation. The kids and the adults left behind were concerned, of course, and hearing that Lena had developed diabetes did not reassure them. Garrett provided some basic information to help the kids cope, but Susannah worried about what would happen when Lena returned to camp. Travis's mother was a diabetic and kept a very strict diet. What did that mean? How should Lena be eating now?

A library would have the answer, and she was familiar with the one in Buffalo, having taken Nathan and Amber there when they lived nearby. All she had to do was get there.

Wednesday afternoon, Susannah gathered her courage and went searching for Wyatt. She found him in the dining room with Amber, where a sheet had been laid over the table and set with cups and saucers, a plate of oatmeal cookies and a pitcher of orange juice. They were, evidently, having a tea party.

"Come sit down, Mommy." Amber got up and pulled out the chair next to her. "You can have some tea, too. It's orange tea," she explained. "Very good."

"Thank you very much." She couldn't catch Wyatt's eye. So she used the only leverage she had. "I'd love to have tea with you, but I wanted to talk to Mr. Wyatt for a few minutes first. Can he be excused?"

Amber rolled her eyes. "If you have to."

Left no choice, Wyatt got to his feet. Susannah led him into the living room.

"Something wrong?" he said when she turned to face him.

Yes, she wanted to say. *You're not talking to me.* Instead, she shook her head. "Oh, no. But I wondered if, when I go to the grocery store tomorrow, I could use your truck to visit the library in Buffalo. I want to find some books on what diabetics should eat."

Brows lowered, he stared at her without answering for so long that she began to get nervous. "Or maybe I could get Dylan to take me…" She'd driven his truck often enough this summer, but something must have changed.

"The truck isn't a problem." He lifted an eyebrow. "What about the internet?"

"Um…what about it?"

"There's plenty of information on the internet about diabetes. That's what Garrett's been reading these last few days."

Susannah swallowed. "I'm pretty rusty as far as computers go. Travis never wanted to spend the money on one. And I… I left school before my senior year. When we ran away."

"You didn't graduate?"

She shook her head, feeling her cheeks heat up.

Wyatt grinned at her for the first time in days. "That makes two of us, doesn't it? But that doesn't have to keep you from using the internet for research. I'll get you started—"

"Mommy!" Amber called. "What's taking so long?"

Wyatt's expression became rueful. "After tea, I guess."

"The princess awaits," Susannah said with a touch of embarrassment. "I'm beginning to think I've spoiled her."

"She's just a five-year-old," he assured her. "Dylan believed he ran the household when he was five." He chuckled. "Some days, he still does."

They returned to the dining room together, laughing. Susannah sat down across from Wyatt, with Amber in between them, and the three of them conducted an intricate conversation at a five-year-old level. To Susannah's delight, Wyatt offered ready answers to her daughter's endless questions—Who lives on the moon? Why is the sky blue? What are clouds made of?—providing explanations that a little girl could understand.

He'll make a wonderful father one day. Nate and Amber would love him to death.

At that moment she'd been pretending to take a sip of "tea," and Susannah gasped at the thought, inhaling a dollop of juice. Choking, with Amber patting her back, she was glad of a legitimate reason for her face to be red.

Wyatt started out of his chair, but she waved for him to sit down. "Are you okay?" he asked.

Still coughing, she nodded. "Really," she sputtered when she saw his anxious expression.

He stood up. "I'll get some water."

Susannah recovered as the dining room door swung

shut behind her. Wiping her eyes, she finally took a deep breath and a clear swallow, just as a knock sounded from the front porch. Thinking Wyatt might not have heard, she went to the screen door…and jerked to a halt.

"Travis," she whispered, her hands at her throat. With a glance behind her, she stepped closer to the doorway. "What are you doing here?" She kept her voice down, so Amber wouldn't hear.

"Hey, babe." He wore a crisp red shirt and new jeans, his hair was cut and he'd shaved recently. "You look beautiful, as always. How are you?"

"You can't be here, Travis. The order of protection says you're to stay away."

He held out his hands. "Aw, come on, Susie. I can't stay away from you. Not to mention my kids. How's my little girl doing? And Nate?"

"You have to leave."

"I'm sorry, Susie. You know I am." He put his hands on the screen and peered inside. "Come out and talk to me. Let me see how you're doing."

If she didn't go out, he would try to come inside. She didn't want him to go anywhere near Amber.

She pulled open the screen door. He didn't move away, standing almost on the threshold. Too close. "Back up," she said. "Please."

Putting up his hands in a gesture of surrender, he stepped sideways. Susannah moved to stand on the other side of the door. "What do you want, Travis? Why did you come?"

"'Cause I want my family back, that's why. I miss you." Driving his hands into his pockets, he hung his head. "Look, I know I've hurt you. I—I start drinking and I just get to feeling so bad because things haven't turned out like they were supposed to. I've taken those feelings out on you, which is wrong because none of this is your fault. You've been the best wife there could be."

He glanced up, and his eyes shone with tears. "I want to start over, make things right. I want to be the best kind of husband and daddy there could be—dependable and considerate. I love you, babe. Come back to me. I'm begging you."

"Have you stopped drinking?"

"I have." When she frowned skeptically, he said, "I swear. I haven't had a drop since the night you left. I'm serious about this, Susie. I need my family. I'll do whatever it takes."

She wanted to be convinced, wanted to believe that they could have a life together without harsh words and blows, without fear and anger. Maybe they could make it work. Maybe he would change this time, really change.

Travis came close, caught her hands in his. "Please, Susie, honey. Let's go home together. Right now. You don't belong with these strangers. You belong to me."

To. One little word. And it made all the difference.

WYATT PUSHED THROUGH the swinging door into the dining room. "Here's a glass—"

Susannah wasn't there. Amber stood on the threshold to the living room, peeking around the corner.

He set the glass down. "What's going on?"

Amber looked over her shoulder. "It's him. He's out there. With Mommy."

The dread on her face was explanation enough. Wyatt put his hands on the little girl's shoulders and steered her into the dining room. "You stay in here with Honey," he said, keeping his voice low. "Don't come out. I'll take care of your mom."

When she nodded, he gave her a wink. "It'll be okay. I promise."

Standing in the living room, fists clenched, he listened without shame as Bradley promised to reform and pleaded for Susannah to come back. Would she buy this load of bull?

"I can't," she said. "I won't. I don't belong *to* you or anyone else. I'm not property. I've spent thirteen years trying to justify a decision I made when I was seventeen. I want to get on with my life, with my children's lives. I'm not going anywhere with you, Travis. And you have to leave. Now." She paused. "Or else I'll call the sheriff."

Wyatt smiled.

Out on the porch, Travis Bradley swore. "I'm doing everything I can to make things right. You ought to respect that and cooperate. We're still married, Susannah. You owe me—"

"I don't owe you anything."

"You owe me those kids. They're mine and I've got a right to see them if I want to."

"The law says you don't."

"I don't give a damn what the law says. You're gonna listen to me."

Wyatt didn't wait to hear more. The screen door slammed behind him when he stepped outside.

Bradley's hands gripped Susannah's shoulders as he held her up against him. He looked around at the noise of the screen. "What the hell—"

Wyatt grabbed his shoulders, wrenched him away and threw him off the porch.

"Get off my property," he ordered. "Don't ever come here again."

Bradley lay on his back on the ground, shaking his head in a daze.

With a snort, Wyatt came after him. "Get your butt up and get out of here." Taking hold of one arm, he dragged the guy upright and sent him stumbling toward his truck. A sharp twinge in his spine warned Wyatt he'd done too much.

Some hero he was.

But Bradley was even less of one. The bastard waited to retaliate until he could put the safety of the vehicle between himself and Wyatt. "You'll see me again," he yelled. "And I'm gonna get those kids. I swear it."

When Wyatt started across the yard, Bradley jumped into his truck and slammed the door. The engine sputtered and choked before it finally caught. In a whirl of dust, Bradley reversed in a circle, slammed into gear and raced down the drive.

Turning toward the house, Wyatt found Susannah standing in the corner of the porch, arms wrapped around her waist. When he reached her, he saw she was shaking. Her face was pale, her eyes squeezed shut.

His voice as gentle as he could make it, he said, "Bradley's gone. Everything's okay."

She didn't move or speak, just stood motionless except for the trembling.

"Are you alright?" He looked her up and down. "Did he hurt you?"

"No," she whispered. After a few seconds, she said, "It's so cold."

She might be in shock. A blanket would help, but he hated to leave her alone.

Raising his hands, he started to cup her shoulders and then hesitated. Should he touch her? Would she understand he just wanted to help? What if she panicked?

"Susannah…" He set his palms lightly on her upper arms. "You can relax. It's alright."

When she didn't react, he curved his fingers to hold on. "Amber's fine. You'll be fine. We'll take care of everything."

Suddenly, she gasped and, covering her face with her hands, began to sob.

Without thinking, Wyatt put his arms around her and pulled her close. He patted her on the shoulder and stroked her hair, the way he would a distraught child. "It's okay," he murmured over and over.

Then he realized *she* was saying something. He bent his head to listen and realized she was whispering, "I'm sorry. So sorry…"

Since she didn't seem to be in any shape to reason with, he just stood there, letting her cry. He'd taken off his brace this morning, which explained the ache in his spine after the brawl with Bradley. But he was glad he'd done it; he couldn't imagine offering much comfort with that thing in the way.

Instead, he could feel her face pressed against his breastbone, her tears wetting his shirt. Her sobs subsided, but her body still shook when she drew a breath. She'd been carrying a lot of pain around with her. Wyatt stayed still as she released it.

Standing there, he noticed that the top of her head came just to his chin. Her shiny gold hair smelled simply clean, without any sweet, fancy scent. Under his hands, the muscles over her ribs felt firm and smooth. His mind's eye showed him her figure, the slender curve of her hips, the roundness of her bottom, the slim length of her legs. Her flat stomach was tucked against his jeans, the swell of her breasts a sweet pressure over his ribs.

Desire crept in, quietly coiling, stealthily insinuating need into his blood, his bones, his belly. Wyatt fought to keep his hands still, his breathing even, as the ache grew more intense. Without success, he tried to evade the mirages his brain showed him—her soft mouth yielding to his, her skin sleek and damp under his palms. His body reacted as he'd feared it would.

Susannah had gone quiet in his arms. He didn't move, aware of her as he had never been aware of another person, wanting to give her all of himself, resisting with every ounce of his control.

After an eternity, she shifted and pulled away slightly. Her gaze was fixed on her hands, which rested on his chest. Wyatt found himself holding his breath, so he wouldn't encourage her to step away. He waited to find out what she was thinking, feeling. Had she sensed his passion? Did she share it?

On the other end of the porch, the screen door squeaked open. "Mommy?"

"Amber." In an instant, Susannah had spun out of his hold and was halfway to the door. "Hey, sweetie. Everything's okay." She swept the little girl up in her arms and stepped inside. "Let's go get the dining room straightened up and start cooking dinner. How does that sound? You can help me make the potato casserole…" Her voice receded as they went into the house.

Wyatt turned toward the corner post of the porch and braced his hands against it. His heart was pounding, his breathing short, as if he'd run the hundred-yard dash.

He cared about Susannah Bradley. Not just with neighborly concern, not friendship or compassion or casual affection. All these weeks, he'd been convinced he could see her every day and stay unmoved by her serene beauty and her gentle, yet determined, character.

Instead, the worst possible thing had happened—he had fallen for Susannah, drawn to her in a way he hadn't experienced in a long, long time. She was married, for God's sake. How much more of a stop sign did it take?

And even if she hadn't been, he couldn't impose his attention on a woman under his protection, especially one who was working for him. She might feel obligated to respond, afraid that if she didn't he would kick her and Amber out, leaving them without a place to go and vulnerable to that bastard Travis Bradley.

A woman coming out of a bad relationship needed time to recover, to stand on her own before considering whether or not she even wanted a man in her life. Wyatt couldn't—wouldn't—pressure Susannah into a connection she was not ready for.

As for himself, he'd been down this road before, with Marley, and he'd sworn not to go there again. Susannah had plans for herself and her kids that did not include him or the Circle M. And his commitment to Henry MacPherson would keep him on the ranch until his dying breath.

Whether that was what he wanted or not.

Chapter Four

"Don't forget to wash your hands," Susannah called as Amber headed for the bathroom. Then she put down the potato she'd started to shred, braced the heels of her hands on the counter and let her head hang between her shoulders.

She couldn't believe what had just happened. Standing on the front porch, for all the world to see, she'd burrowed into Wyatt, seeking…what? Protection? He'd given her that. Comfort? Consolation? He'd offered all she could ask. She should have been grateful for the support provided by a friend. She should have stepped away.

But she'd found herself wanting more. His big, warm hands spread across her back made her aware of herself in a way she hadn't been for years. She'd imagined those hands moving over her skin, and she shivered with anticipation. His heart beating against her ear set up a strange new rhythm for her pulse, urging her closer, rousing a need she hadn't imagined she could still experience.

She wasn't a fool—she could tell his body had responded to hers. Men were more susceptible to physical cues than women, and she didn't blame him. But thank God for Amber! If her little girl hadn't interrupted, Susannah might have looked up at Wyatt with her feelings written on her face. She might have begged him for a kiss.

And what a mistake that would have been. Kissing Wyatt would release emotions she'd been trying very hard to ignore—a concern and a caring that came perilously close to love.

The thud of his boot heels in the dining room warned her to straighten up and get her face arranged. She had just grabbed the grater again when he came into the kitchen.

Susannah glanced up with a smile but didn't let her gaze connect with his. Given what had happened on the porch, it was the best she could do.

He cleared his throat. "Where's Amber?"

"In the bathroom." Hearing his stern tone, she raised her head. "Is something wrong?"

"I wanted to talk to you. I'm glad she's not here."

"There is something wrong."

Coming closer, he leaned a hip against the counter. "You should call the sheriff and report that Bradley turned up here. Deputy Wade Daughtrey's a friend of ours—he'll be glad to help out. Your husband violated the order of protection and harassed you. Daughtrey ought to be aware of that."

With a shake of her head, she resumed grating. "No, I don't think so."

"Why not?"

She sighed. "If the sheriff comes after him, he'll get even more upset, and who knows what he'll do then? He didn't hurt anyone today. Unless..." Now she stared at him, suddenly worried. "Are you alright? You don't have your brace on and you grabbed him and—and... Did you hurt your back?"

"I'm fine. Didn't feel a twinge."

He avoided her eyes, so she couldn't decide if he was telling the truth. "If he thinks he can come out here without consequences, he might try again."

When she only shook her head, Wyatt got exasperated. "I don't understand why you haven't sued for divorce and kicked this guy out of your life once and for all."

Her hands went still. After a moment, she looked up at him. "I did file for divorce. The day he was served the papers, he went out drinking. When he came home, he started hitting me. And Nate. That was the night you took us in. You saw what happened today when I defied him. If you hadn't been here, hadn't intervened…"

She swallowed the remembered fear. "That's why I don't intend to challenge him again."

"It's not right. How long—"

"And don't tell Ford. He'll want to get involved."

"But—"

Amber skipped into the kitchen, holding up her hands. "All clean, Mommy. See?"

"Good job. We're almost ready to mix the potatoes." Holding Wyatt's gaze, she shrugged. "That's the best I can do for now."

Hands propped on his hips, he blew out a sigh. "Yeah. I guess so." Then he sent Amber a wink. "See you later, alligator."

Her favorite rhyme. "In a while, crocodile," she crowed and then giggled as he waved and left the room.

Susannah blew out a sigh of her own. With half her mind on Amber and their dinner preparations, she realized she'd forgotten all about Lena's food requirements and her plan to work out healthy menus for a teenager with diabetes. After dinner with the teenagers, there were ball games in the yard in front of the ranch house, another of Amber's favorite things. She loved getting the chance to play with her brother, and the other kids were kind enough to include her in their activities. Susannah watched from the porch, trying not to recall the afternoon's incident with Travis, trying to avoid Wyatt's gaze and the memory of those few moments in his arms.

Darkness brought bath time for Amber, followed by a story and the inevitable argument about going to bed. Susannah finally closed the door to their room about nine o'clock, exhausted with the emotional effort.

She jumped when she realized Wyatt stood just across the hallway, hands in his pockets, leaning one shoulder against the wall.

"That's quite an effort, getting her to sleep," he said. "You'd think she'd be tired."

"The more tired she is, the harder she fights." Susannah brushed strands of hair away from her face. She probably looked a mess. "She's battling herself as much as me."

He gave a brief snort. "Who isn't?"

What did that mean? Susannah glanced at his face but didn't find him smiling. Swallowing hard, she steeled herself to be practical. "Is tonight still okay for doing some work on the computer?" She would have preferred to keep more distance between them, but the needs of others came first. "Garrett says Lena will be back from the hospital soon. I'd like to be ready for her."

After a long moment, he straightened up. "Sure."

Following him down the passage, she couldn't help letting her eyes linger on his broad shoulders, his long legs and narrow hips. Without the brace, he seemed hale and hearty, the classic image of a hardworking cowboy—strong and determined and too sexy to be close to.

Yet here she was going into his bedroom.

"I brought in an extra chair. Have a seat." Sitting beside her, he propped an elbow on the desk. "So, have you ever used a computer?"

"Lately only at the library," she said, twisting her hands together in her lap. "The catalogs are all in the computer now." He had switched on several lamps, but the shadows along the walls made the room seem small. Intimate.

Wyatt didn't appear to be affected by the atmosphere. "This isn't much different. You just search for whatever you're interested in. Such as *diabetes diet*. This is what you do." He reached over to type on the keyboard in front of her, brushing her arm with his. "Hit return and—bang—you get all these listings with the information you want."

Susannah focused on the screen. "Is that *millions* of listings?"

His mouth quirked into a grin. "Yep."

They were awfully close together, his knee just inches from her thigh. "Incredible." Her palms were damp with nerves.

A few clicks took her to a page with useful information she wanted to save. She started to ask for pen and paper, but then she hesitated. "Can I just print this off?"

Her reward was another grin. "This page has a printer symbol up in the corner. Click there." A whirring noise from the printer to her left heralded a sheaf of papers, produced in just seconds. "There's your information."

"Great." She went back to the search page for more listings. "I can't believe what I've missed. You could find almost anything you wanted on the Internet."

He chuckled. "You can *buy* almost anything you want."

She widened her eyes. "Anything?"

Standing up, he gazed down at her. "Groceries,

clothes, books, furniture…you could probably buy yourself a private airplane, if you wanted. Or a yacht. You
must have seen the ads on TV."

Her cheeks heated with a blush. "Our sets were always secondhand and usually didn't work very well, so
I never paid much attention to commercials. We couldn't
afford cable service, didn't have computers or fancy
phones. Just the basics."

"But even with minimum TV—"

"The kids and I watched their shows on public TV,
or videotapes. You can find lots of those in the thrift
stores. When he was home, Travis tuned in to sports,
but we were usually in another room because he would
be getting drunk." Now her whole face felt hot. "Nathan
took classes in computers at school, but since we didn't
have one…" She shrugged. "He did his homework before he came home."

"Well, now you know what to do." He walked to the
door. "I'll leave you to surf to your heart's content. Have
fun."

The clock in the corner of the screen said eleven thirty
when Susannah finally slumped against the chair and
rubbed her eyes. She'd printed out a stack of paper about
an inch thick—between her computer use and Amber's
art projects, she should buy Wyatt a pack of paper very
soon. But she had a much better understanding of the
meals they should provide for Lena to stay healthy. In
fact, all the kids could use less sugar and starch in their
diets, more fruit, vegetables and whole grains.

Gathering her research, she went to tell Wyatt she'd
finished. He sat in the rocking chair in the living room
with a book, of course, and Honey curled up at his feet.
The dog thumped her tail as Susannah came in but otherwise didn't move.

Wyatt glanced up from his pages. "You found what you wanted?"

She held up her pages. "I could have kept going all night. But I have enough information to get started. Thanks for bringing me into the twenty-first century."

"You're more than welcome. Feel free to use the computer anytime."

Something about the night or her mood—or maybe the warmth in his dark brown eyes—brought a confession to the surface. "I feel pretty stupid, being so far behind the rest of the world. I'm determined that at least Nathan and Amber will get a good education." She gave a wry laugh. "Though how my parents could have stopped me from running away, I don't know. Maybe if they'd accepted Travis, instead of trying to keep us apart…"

"You're not stupid," Wyatt said in a stern voice. "But it bothers you, not graduating from high school?"

Lips pressed together, she nodded.

"Me, too. That's why I earned my GED. It's the equivalent of a high school diploma for going to college or getting a job."

Susannah huffed a frustrated breath. "Something else I'm not caught up on."

He frowned at her. "No discouragement allowed. As your computer instructor, I'm giving you an assignment—look it up. Go to the computer and find out about the GED. Then we'll talk."

An hour later she returned with more papers and dropped down onto the sofa. "Four tests! I can't possibly pass four tests. Social Studies? Science? Math? Not to mention I haven't written an essay since before Nathan was born."

He marked the page in his book and closed it. "You'll

have to study. And you don't have to take the tests all at once. But you could do it, Susannah. If you want to."

"Why do you think so?"

"Because you're a survivor. You've come out of a bad situation, and you intend to make a better life for yourself and your kids. The GED is a step in that direction and not even the hardest one. You've already taken the hardest step."

As she held his gaze, Susannah's heart lurched in a tug of war between doubt and hope.

Since she'd cut herself off from her family, she'd concentrated on what Travis wanted and then, of course, what her children needed. As her marriage unraveled, as life became a struggle to cope, she'd learned to ignore her own needs. Her own dreams. But Wyatt said she could do it. A man who was so skilled, so intelligent and responsible believed in her ability to improve her life beyond basic survival. He wanted more for her.

Did she want more for herself?

"You're right," she told him as hope won the struggle for her heart. "It might take me a while, with all the studying. There are courses I can take to prepare, but they're pretty expensive."

"I'll float you a loan," Wyatt said and got to his feet. "I'm betting you're good for it."

Susannah fell in love with him at that moment.

She couldn't tell him so, of course—she was, as a matter of fact, still married. And her messy life wasn't the place a man like Wyatt wanted to be.

Just knowing the truth, on her own, would have to be enough.

And so she got to her feet and mirrored his confident smile. "I'm betting you're right."

August

THEY ALL LOOKED pretty funny in their swimsuits.

Becky sat on the side of the pool, kicking her legs in the water and watching the other kids play Marco Polo. They'd spent the summer riding horses and wearing jeans, so their legs and stomachs were pale compared to their arms and faces.

Of course, the girls couldn't exactly show off anyway, because of the stupid tank suits Ms. Caroline had bought them—they might as well be a swim team, since they were all navy blue. One size definitely did not fit everyone—Lena was a little too skinny, especially since she'd been diagnosed with diabetes, while Becky knew that her hips were too wide, her legs too chubby. It didn't help that her arms and cheeks were still splotchy from peeling after that sunburn a few weeks ago. And then there were the freckles, everywhere…

But Lizzie was pretty no matter what she wore, and the blue suit was no exception. Tall, with long, pretty legs, bright blond hair and big blue eyes, she didn't need the makeup she put on to look sexy. Her boobs were big enough and her butt filled out her jeans—as well as the suit—just right. Her skin went from pale to tan without a burn. No freckles.

And the boys had noticed. Well, except for Justino, who never really saw anyone except Lena. Thomas and Marcos, though, were circling around Lizzie like sharks as she kept her eyes closed and tried to find them in the water, calling "Marco! Marco!" and listening for their "Polo!" answers. Lizzie understood very well what was going on—she never tried to reach for Lena or Justino, though they were playing, too. Laughing and teasing,

Lizzie searched for the boys, who stayed just far enough away not to get caught.

A hand settled on Becky's shoulder. "Are you feeling okay?" Ms. Caroline sat down beside her. She'd bought herself one of the blue suits, too—so everybody could be miserable together, she'd said—and she was as attractive as Lizzie, even though she was so much older.

"I thought you'd be out there playing."

"Just soaking up some sun." As if she wasn't totally lathered up with sunscreen. "I'm going in right now." Sliding into the cool water, she figured maybe if she got to be It, Nate would remember she was alive. So far, her plan for making him her boyfriend had not been a screaming success.

"Polo!" she yelled, coming within Lizzie's reach.

"Polo!" Thomas floated on the other side, farther away, and Lizzie splashed in his direction.

"Polo!" Becky moved after her best friend, determined to be caught.

"Marco?" Lizzie turned away, toward the boys. She was different these days, sort of far away, as if she and Becky hadn't cut classes together, hadn't cheated off each other's papers and shared hours in detention. As if they hadn't gotten caught smoking dope together, which was what got them sent to this camp to begin with.

"Polo," Becky said again and grabbed her by the arm. "I'm It."

Lizzie opened her eyes to glare. "That's cheating. I didn't catch you, you caught me."

"Oh, let her be It," Lena said. "You've done it long enough."

Sticking her lower lip out, Lizzie started to pout. After a few seconds, though, she gave in. "Fine." She sent a spray of water in Becky's direction. "Who cares, anyway?"

Becky closed her eyes and called, "Marco!" She heard Lena and Justino and the boys, but Lizzie didn't answer. The next time, there were two boys...and then one. After a few minutes, Lena and Justino stopped playing. So she stopped calling, since the game didn't work with just two people.

She opened her eyes to see Lizzie sitting on the ladder at the deep end, with Thomas and Marcos treading water at her feet. Did they realize how ridiculous they were?

Nate had stayed in the game with her, because he was a nice guy. When she glanced at him, though, he was watching Lizzie splashing Thomas and Marcos with her feet. He wanted to be there but wouldn't desert her in the middle of the pool.

Fabulous—she was a pity date.

Stretching out her arm, she slung a wall of water in his direction. "Go on," she said. "I'm tired of this stupid game."

Being a boy, he didn't understand. "What's wrong?"

"Nothing." Thank goodness they were in a pool, in case the tears in her eyes fell out. "Just go away."

He glanced at his mom, sitting at the shallow end with his sister, Amber. Becky hoped for a second he might go that way and actually held her breath.

Instead, he stretched into the water and swam over to the wall beside Lizzie. Now she could splash all three of them.

And if we're lucky, Becky thought, *they'll drown.*

Not that it was a big deal if Nate liked Lizzie, instead of her. Her mom was always saying she was a loser, so she shouldn't be surprised. She wasn't pretty, wasn't smart or talented, and there was no reason a boy—or anyone else, for that matter—would think she was special.

There were only a few weeks left before the end of camp and the beginning of school. They were running out of time to be together.

And Becky had no idea what she could do to get his attention.

WYATT HAD NEVER felt so out of place in his life. No self-respecting cowboy found himself sitting beside a swimming pool in the middle of an August work day—wearing shorts, for God's sake. He hadn't put on a pair of shorts in probably a decade. Maybe longer.

But one of the couples at church had offered Garrett the use of their backyard pool to give the teenagers a change of pace from their usual ranch activities. Then his brothers had ganged up on him, basically forcing him to come along. *Get out of the house for a change, get some sun, get some time with the kids*…they'd bombarded him with a list of benefits he would *get* by joining the swim party. They'd even bought him the shorts.

So here he was, bare legs and feet exposed to the world. At least he'd kept his shirt on. After a summer inside, his usual rancher's tan had faded out of sight. No back brace, though, which was a relief.

"Cheer up, Boss." Carrying a bottle of water in each hand, Ford sat down in the lounge chair beside him, his blond hair dark and sleek from a few quick lengths. "You're supposed to be enjoying yourself." Having lived in California, the family lawyer actually possessed swim trunks to wear at a pool party. "The water's great—you should try it out." He slid one bottle across the table and uncapped the other to take a swig.

Wyatt snorted. "Not likely. I've forded streams and

rivers on horseback, rescued my share of stranded cows from high water. That doesn't mean I enjoy standing around dripping wet."

"I know." His brother grinned at him. "Look at Amber, though. There's nothing cuter than a five-year-old and a pair of water wings. She's loving it."

In fact, Wyatt had been trying hard *not* to watch the little girl playing on the steps at the shallow end of the pool because right beside Amber stood Susannah, keeping a close eye on her daughter. She wore a blue, one-piece swimsuit that was not at all revealing, and yet his pulse kicked up every time he looked at her. Slender curves, smooth skin, long legs...yeah, he had a real problem focusing his attention anywhere else.

"Pretty amazing, when you think about it," Ford said. "At the start of this camp enterprise, we didn't realize we needed someone like Susannah on board. But over the last month or so she's become indispensable."

Wyatt shifted in his chair. "Amazing."

"Caroline and Garrett expected the kids to take care of all their food, their laundry, their housekeeping," his brother continued. "But without Susannah's guidance, they wouldn't have picked up the routines and learned to manage as well as they have."

"Good point."

"Not to mention her cooking. And keeping the house looking like a showplace."

"She's done a great job."

"That order of protection I got her will expire soon. She's going to have to figure out what to do next. Has she said anything to you about what she's thinking?"

"Don't know why she would." He'd been careful to keep Susannah's secrets, even from his brother.

With the persistence of a terrier, Ford wouldn't let the

subject go. "You two have spent a lot of time in the house together, so I thought she might have mentioned it."

"Nope."

"I'm kind of surprised Bradley hasn't shown up at some point this summer, begging her to come back." There was a reason Ford was a top-notch attorney. "He's the type who would hate being told no."

Wyatt didn't reply. He didn't intend to lie if he could help it.

Of course, he'd been deceiving his brothers for twenty years, since the night their dad died. What difference did a few white lies make, compared to a lifetime of dishonesty?

Ford's voice intruded on his thoughts. "She's a lovely lady."

He realized he'd been caught staring at Susannah again. "Yes, she is." There was no point in denying the obvious. "But you're practically a married man."

"So is she. Married, that is."

"I'm aware." He shifted his gaze to watch Marcos do a cannonball jump off the diving board.

"The end of a bad relationship isn't a good time to start a new one."

Wyatt unclenched his jaw. "What's your point?"

"Getting involved—"

Rescue arrived from an unexpected direction.

"Come play with me," Amber demanded, standing on the deck in front of him with her blond curls slicked straight, her pink-and-purple-striped swimsuit dripping onto his bare toes. "I want to jump in."

Wyatt stalled. "Why?"

"They all do it." She nodded toward the teenagers in the deep end. At that moment, her brother took a leap off the side of the pool, feet first. "See? It's fun."

"And why do you need me?"

"You're the strongest one here. You have to catch me."

"Have you done this before?"

The little girl nodded. "Lots of times."

He glanced beyond her and saw Susannah and Caroline unpacking snacks on the patio table. "What does your mother say about this plan?"

"It's okay," Amber said. "Please?"

What could he say to that? He got to his feet and held out a hand. "Let's go, Princess."

"Wait a second," Ford said. "Do you think that's a good idea? Your back—"

He threw a glare over his shoulder and kept walking. About halfway along the length of the pool, he stopped. "Is this a good spot for jumping?"

Amber peered over the edge, and nodded. "It's deep enough." Then she frowned at him. "Silly, you can't wear your shirt in the water."

He'd forgotten about the shirt. "I guess not." He pulled it over his head and tossed it on the nearby lounge chair, ignoring his own discomfort. "Okay?"

"Okay!" She clapped her hands. "Are you going to dive in?"

"No. Never dive in the shallow end." He sat down on the side and put his feet in, wincing. "It's cold."

"Not after a minute," Amber assured him. "Get in so I can jump."

"Right." Wyatt slid into the water. Great—now he had a ghost-pale, goose-bump-covered chest. "How far out are you going to jump?"

"A long, long way."

He backed halfway across the pool. "Here?"

She motioned him to come toward her. "There."

"Okay. You ready?"

All at once, Amber looked a little worried. But she nodded.

Holding out his arms, he said, "I'll catch you. One… two…three!"

She bent her knees and froze. "Come closer."

He stepped up to a point about a yard off the wall. "Now?"

"Okay."

He counted off again. This time she jumped and landed on top of him, her arms in a stranglehold around his neck.

"Good job," he managed, his arms under her bottom. "You jumped."

She sat back and grinned at him. "I jumped!"

"Amber Bradley, just what do you think you're doing?" Suddenly, Susannah stood above them, glaring down, hands on her hips.

"I jumped, Mommy! Did you see?"

Wyatt suddenly had the feeling he'd been conned. "She said—"

"What did I tell you, Amber? What did I say?"

Her daughter mumbled something even Wyatt couldn't hear.

Susannah didn't relent. "I can't hear you."

This answer was clearer. "Not to bother Mr. Wyatt."

"Why?"

"Because you didn't want me to jump."

Moving to the wall, Wyatt set the little girl on her feet on top. "It's okay. We won't do it again."

"That is not the point." Susannah bent over to look Amber directly in the face. "You did exactly what I told you not to. And you lied to Mr. Wyatt. I am very disappointed in you, Amber Bradley." She started to deflate the water wings on Amber's arms.

"No, Mommy, don't! I want to swim."

Susannah shook her head. "You're done for the day." Removing the wings, she took Amber by the hand and led her to a chair in the shade of the deck awning. Making his way to the steps in the shallow water, Wyatt couldn't hear her words, but he got the general idea when Amber burst into tears.

He was picking up his shirt when Susannah marched up to him. "Sorry about that," he said. "I didn't—"

"Why didn't you ask me?" she demanded, arms crossed over her chest. "You should have checked with me before taking her into the pool."

"She told me—"

"She's five. She'll say whatever it takes to get her way."

"Right. I didn't think." He figured the safest way out of this was to just agree with what she said.

But Susannah wasn't finished. "She could have been hurt."

He tried to reassure her. "I wasn't going to let that happen."

"You might have been hurt. You have a broken back, remember? What if you'd had a sudden pain and couldn't hold her?"

"I didn't. My back is fine. I wouldn't have—"

"I'll believe that when the doctor says so," she said sharply. "Until then, you shouldn't take such risks, especially with Amber."

So much for making peace. "I understand." Now he was glaring, too. The noise around them had died away.

"I hope so. Now I have to go deal with my daughter before she ruins the party for everyone else." Turning on her heel, she went over to Amber, who was still wailing from her chair on the deck.

From the other side of the pool, Garrett broke the uneasy silence among the kids. "Hey, guys, we've got snacks set out. Dry off and come get some food."

Wyatt headed away from the stampede, toward the chair he'd occupied before this fiasco had started. He pulled his shirt over his head and then sat down.

Ford leaned forward, mouth open to say something.

"Don't start." He held up a hand. "Just let it be." They weren't too far from Amber to hear her sniffles and the quiet murmur of Susannah's voice.

"You don't tangle with Mama Bear," his brother said anyway.

"I'll remember that," Wyatt snapped. "Believe me, I'll remember."

Chapter Five

Amber fell asleep in the van on the return to the ranch. Dylan, who had napped on a lounge chair during most of the party, carried her into the house and set her down on the bed in his former bedroom. "Swimming wears me out, too," he commented.

Susannah knew it was the tears that had made her girl sleepy. "I'll wake her up in a little while. Or else she'll be up till midnight."

"I'll take your word for that," he said with a grin. "A mom knows."

With her clothes changed and her hair dried, she went into the kitchen to start dinner. She found a new pot of coffee steaming in the machine but no sign of the maker. It must have been Wyatt. He'd poured his coffee and then gone away, avoiding her.

Susannah was planning to apologize. He was her employer, after all. You didn't yell at your boss if you wanted to keep your job.

More important, he was a friend. Someone she cared about, someone she didn't want to hurt. Especially when she'd overreacted. She'd have to find him and explain.

"Hey, Susannah." Caroline stepped into the kitchen, followed by Ford. "Do you have a few minutes?"

"Of course. What can I do for you? Would you like

some coffee?" She poured each of them a cup and they sat down around the kitchen table. "This looks serious," she joked…sort of. Had Wyatt sent them to fire her?

"I wanted to talk with you about your plans." Ford held his mug in both hands, his elbows propped on the table. "The order of protection we filed will expire soon. Have you decided what to do about that? How you want to proceed?"

"I want a divorce," she told him. "I can't live with Travis again."

Caroline nodded. "I think that's the right choice, for your safety as well as Nate and Amber's."

"I can handle that for you," Ford said. "There shouldn't be a problem, even if he contests it."

"Does it make a difference if I've already filed?" She explained what had set Travis off that night. "I haven't pursued it—I wasn't sure what to do. Or maybe—" she took a deep breath "—maybe I was just avoiding the whole issue." She'd felt safe this summer, with Wyatt, with the Marshall brothers and Caroline. Ignoring the reason she was there had been too easy.

"Well." Frowning, Ford gazed into his drink. "I'll have to check on the status of your file, find out where the paperwork is in the process. I must say, you're better off having an attorney to represent you, since you have children to consider. From what I've seen, Bradley is likely to contest the divorce. Filing for yourself only works if there's no contest."

"I was desperate," she told him. "But I can't afford—"

He waved off her objection. "We'll work something out. I'll be at the courthouse tomorrow and can chase down your petition." Getting to his feet, he took Caroline's cup and his own to the dishwasher. "I mentioned to Wyatt this afternoon that I'm surprised Bradley hasn't shown up this summer, trying to see you or the kids. He didn't seem the type to give up so easily. Of course, that would be a good thing…" Turning around, he saw the blush she could feel heating up her face. "Or has he been here?"

Susannah nodded.

"You should have called the sheriff's department. How did you get him to leave?"

"Wyatt—"

She didn't have to explain further. Ford glanced at Caroline and nodded. "Too bad. Having that violation documented could have been useful in the divorce proceedings. Now it's just she-said, he-said. Wyatt should have realized that."

"I asked him not to report it. Travis gets so angry. I was worried about what he would do."

Caroline put a hand over hers on the table. "That's understandable. Is it too late?" she asked Ford. "He wouldn't have waited around for the sheriff anyway."

"We can always try." Coming back to the table, Ford put a hand on Susannah's shoulder. "We'll work this out and secure your divorce. You deserve to live a life without fear."

"More than that," Caroline said, "you deserve the life you want. We'll help you any way we can."

"Thank you so much." She blotted the tears on the sleeve of her shirt. "I just want my children to be safe and happy."

"But what about you?" Caroline asked, after Ford left. "What do you want for yourself?"

Standing at the counter, Susannah paused, her knife poised over a cucumber. "I…" She frowned. "I'm not sure."

Caroline took a sip of coffee. "What were you planning, in high school? What were your interests?"

Frowning, she tried to remember those days as a teenager before Travis sauntered down the hallway at school and took her breath away. She must have had some sort of goals, some vision of the future. "My parents wanted me to go to college and then teach, like they did. I remember I thought that sounded dull." She chuckled. "I know better now, after two children."

"You still could," Caroline said. "Wyoming can always use good teachers."

Susannah nodded. "I've started studying for my GED. At this rate, though, it will take me a long time to finish. Meanwhile, I suspect I'll be working somewhere that doesn't require a diploma—as a cashier in a store, maybe, or a server in a restaurant. But I'll look for something more permanent as soon as I can."

And that was the answer, she decided after Caroline had gone and she moved around the kitchen getting dinner together. More than anything else, what she wanted for her children and for herself was stability. For so long, they'd been at the mercy of Travis's whims, his mistakes and his carelessness. She wanted to build a life they could count on, day after day—the same home, the same school, the same job. A neighborhood they were familiar with, a playground or ball field where they could get to know people. A church where they could feel loved.

The kind of life she'd had growing up.

Maybe even including…grandparents? If she worked hard enough, proved herself, would her parents let her—and her children—into their lives?

Susannah knew she had to make that happen. Even with a divorce, Travis would always be a factor in their lives. But, despite him, she would find a way to give Nathan and Amber the sense of well-being she recalled from her own childhood, the confidence that everything would be alright. As their mother, she owed them that much. She owed it to herself.

With dinner almost ready, she woke Amber and coaxed her into the shower to wash the chlorine out of her hair. Then they had a long talk. At seven, clean and neatly dressed, they were sitting in the dining room when Wyatt's footsteps sounded in the hall.

He stopped in the doorway, frowning. "What's going on? Am I late?"

Eyebrows raised, Susannah looked at her daughter, who heaved a sigh and slid out of her chair.

Standing in front of Wyatt, she gazed up into his face. "I'm sorry I told you a lie, Mr. Wyatt. That's not a nice thing to do, 'specially not to a friend. I won't do it again. I want you to be my friend."

His face softened. "Thanks for the apology, Amber. I want to be your friend." He held out his hand. "Let's shake on it."

Amber took his hand and pumped it enthusiastically. Then she looked at Susannah. "Can we eat now?"

"Get into your chair." To Wyatt, she said, "Would you help me bring in the food?" She didn't usually make that request, so she wasn't surprised at his puzzled expression. But he followed her into the kitchen.

Only a few steps in, she turned to face him. "I want to apologize, as well."

He was closer than she'd anticipated, an arm's length away. His frown was back.

"You should have checked with me before letting Amber jump into the pool, but I shouldn't have yelled at you."

After a long silence, he said, "I thought you trusted me."

"I do." More than anyone she'd ever known. "But…" She drew a deep breath. "I can't swim. I'm not afraid of the water, exactly, but my mother was, so I never learned. Nate has taken lessons, and Amber will, too. I haven't let her jump in before because there was no one to catch her, so it made me nervous when I saw what was happening. I took that out on you. And I'm sorry."

"It's okay." Out came the smile she loved. "You should learn to swim, too. Take some lessons."

She held up her hands, laughing. "Let me get my GED first, why don't you? I can only take in so much at one time."

"Oh, I think you underestimate yourself." Wyatt was laughing, too. Maybe, as she was, out of relief that they weren't at odds anymore?

Their laughter died away, but their gazes held, smiling yet intent. Susannah found herself holding her breath, not sure what was happening. To her surprise, Wyatt's hand came to her cheek, lightly resting against her skin.

"You're so beautiful when you laugh," he said, his voice low.

Without thinking, she leaned her head into his palm. He drew a quick breath.

The screen door slammed. "Mom! Hey, Mom!"

In an instant, they stood yards apart.

But even if they hadn't moved, Nathan had only one thing on his mind.

"Is the ice cream ready yet?"

THAT NIGHT—FOR ONCE—Lizzie didn't complain to Becky about coming inside at bedtime.

"A dance. Can you believe it?" She whirled around and then fell spread-eagle backward onto the double bed. "We're going to have a dance!"

Lena went to stare in the mirror over the dresser, finger combing her long, straight black hair. "Mr. Garrett told me we would, when I went to the hospital. He said I could teach him to salsa."

As excited as her friends, Becky sat on the corner of their bed that Lizzie left free. "Who gets to choose the music?"

"We do, of course," Lizzie said. "I've got it all in my phone. Hours and hours."

Becky thought about Nate. "The boys might want to pick some of the songs, too."

Lizzie waved that idea away. "They don't care. Anyway, we'll have to make them dance."

"Not Justino," Lena said. "He loves to dance." She grinned. "With me, of course."

On the bed, Lizzie was now doing leg lifts, barely missing hitting Becky in the head. "It'll be so cool— a dance floor outside, with lights strung up around it. What other decorations could we do?"

"Balloons?" Becky said. "Helium-filled, so they float."

"Balloons," Lizzie said, "are for babies."

Becky stuck her tongue out but was ignored.

Lena began brushing her hair. She did a hundred strokes every night. "I like balloons. Red and black ones would be sophisticated."

"Invisible in the dark" was Lizzie's verdict. "I guess we could do glow-in-the-dark balloons," she conceded. "I wish we could have a disco ball."

"How would you hang it—from the sky?" Becky asked. "And how are you going to make Thomas and Marco dance? They'll probably just stand around eating."

"What are we going to eat?" Lena asked. "Do we have to do the cooking?" Food was Lena's favorite subject these days because she was always hungry and had to watch what she ate.

"Cupcakes," Lizzie said. "Chips and salsa. Pizza for the main course."

"I'm not supposed to eat any of that," Lena complained. "Think about somebody besides yourself for a change."

Lizzie rolled her eyes. "Well, what do you want to eat? Celery and broiled chicken?"

"Maybe we need a theme," Becky said in desperation. "To help us make plans."

"That's right. A theme." Lizzie considered for a few seconds. "I've got it. We could have a beach party."

Now Lena rolled her eyes. "You're always about the beach. And you've never even been there."

"Neither have you," Lizzie shot back.

"So we don't know anything about beaches," Lena said, still brushing. "What are we gonna do? Throw sand everywhere?"

Lizzie sat up, flipping her hair behind her shoulders in the way she did when she was mad. "We could have everybody wear flip-flops and shorts. And decorate with beach balls. Beach chairs. Inflatable palm trees. There's lots of stuff that would be fun."

"Lame," Lena said.

"We're on a ranch," Becky suggested quickly. "We could do a barn dance theme. Then we'd have the right clothes to wear—jeans and boots."

"Boring. We've been doing that all summer."

Lena shimmied out of her jeans and into her pajama bottoms. "Fiesta would be a fun theme. We could have a piñata. Tacos and nachos to eat and virgin margaritas to drink. Lots of salsa music."

"That's a cool idea." Becky turned to Lizzie, hoping for a truce. "The guys would like hitting a piñata."

Not a chance. "The point is dancing," Lizzie said, "not beating some stupid puppet with a stick. Who wants to chase after a bunch of candy, anyway? I'd rather have cupcakes."

Lena threw up her hands. "You just want to have everything your way. You never consider anybody but yourself." She pulled her T-shirt over her head. "I'm sick and tired of it."

"You're the one who throws temper tantrums about food," Lizzie told her. "Thanks to you, we hardly ever get cookies or ice cream anymore."

"Come on," Becky pleaded. "Nobody has to get mad. Let's just—"

"I don't care what you do about the stupid dance," Lena shouted. "Justino and I won't even be there. We'll find something else to do that night." She got into bed, pulled up the covers and turned her back to the room.

"Well, I'm not planning it," Lizzie countered. "You all think my ideas are stupid and I don't want to work that hard anyway. I'll just show up and have a good time without doing anything to help." She grabbed her pajamas out from under her pillow and stomped off to the bathroom, where she slammed the door.

"Great." Becky changed into her pajamas and got into bed, though she'd have to get up again when Lizzie finally came out of the bathroom.

In the meantime, she tried to figure out what to do about the dance. Ms. Caroline had said it was up to them to plan the food, though Nate's mom would help with the cooking, if needed. But who was going to decide what kind of food to have, if Lizzie and Lena didn't? What about decorations? Were they necessary? She fell asleep before Lizzie came out of the bathroom and before she had the answers to her questions. She awoke in the morning with dirty teeth and only one idea about the party. Ask Nate.

Their team was cooking breakfast, so she didn't get a chance to talk to him until after the eggs were scrambled, the bacon broiled and the toast buttered. Luckily, there was an empty chair beside him when she'd served her plate.

Sitting down, she took a deep breath and said, "Hi."

His quick glance wasn't exactly encouraging. "Hi."

Her appetite died. "Um…pretty cool about having a dance, huh?"

He shrugged one shoulder. "I guess." After a few seconds, he added, "I've never been to a dance."

Becky gulped. "Me, neither." She crumbled her toast over her eggs. "But Lizzie and Lena had a fight. Neither of them wants to plan it."

He frowned. "What's there to plan?"

Lizzie was right. Boys didn't care. "Food. Music. Decorations." She gathered her courage and said, "You have to help me."

"Why me?"

Because I like you, she thought. *Because I want you to like me and there are only three weeks left before I have to go home and the fairy tale ends.* Before she had to return to a house crammed with junk of every description, where she lived with two women who fought all the time and cared only about themselves.

But she couldn't say that. "Because nobody else will. Marcos and Thomas will just laugh at me if I ask them. I can't do it by myself."

Then he asked the hardest question of all. "Why not?"

She slapped her hands on the table. "Because then we

won't have a dance. And I'll tell Ms. Caroline that it's your fault because you wouldn't help."

He glared at her. "Is that supposed to be blackmail? What are they going to do—tie me to a horse and drag me around?"

"Please, Nate." She didn't have to fake tears. "It'll be fun."

"I doubt it." But then he sighed. "Okay. What is it we're supposed to do, exactly?"

"We'll have a meeting," she told him, grinning. "After lunch, before we go riding. Thanks!" Figuring she'd pushed him far enough, she stood up. "See you then."

To her surprise, he flashed a grin in return. "Right."

Taking her plate to the sink, she felt like dancing. Nate would have to talk to her if they were working together on the dance. And if they spent enough time together, he might decide he liked her more than Lizzie... maybe more than just a friend. Now she had a chance, at least.

On her way to the door, Lizzie caught up with her. "What were you talking to Nate about?"

Cornered, Becky couldn't come up with a good excuse. "The dance."

"What about it?"

"He's going to help me plan it."

Lizzie let her jaw drop. "You? You're going to plan the dance?"

"You said you wouldn't." She shrugged. "Somebody has to. Or else there won't be one."

Eyes narrowed, Lizzie stared at her. "You're supposed to be on my side. You're my friend."

"I can plan the dance and still be your friend."

"You're just trying to get Nate for yourself."

Becky glanced around to check if anybody had heard

her. "That's dumb. He's just one of the guys." Then she said, "You can't have them all."

Lizzie sent her a mocking smile. "Watch me." She sidestepped Becky and went straight to the table where Nate sat and took the chair beside him. In another minute, whatever she'd said made him laugh.

Becky slammed the bunkhouse door as she walked out.

Mr. Dylan was coming up the hill toward her. "Whoa, there. Everything okay? You look a little flustered."

"Sometimes," she said, "you need to fight for what you want."

He nodded. "That's true. If it's worth having." His understanding gaze didn't seem to require more explanation. "You are as important, as valuable, as everybody else."

"Right." Striding toward the barn, she recalled Lizzie's mean expression. *This is war,* she thought. *A war for Nate's heart.*

And I'm going to win.

THURSDAY MORNING, FORD strode into the kitchen as Wyatt was finishing his breakfast. Taking off his hat, he said, "Good morning, Susannah." Then he faced Wyatt. "Boss, I've got bad news."

Wyatt put down his fork. "What's up?"

"I just got a call from Judge Parker's clerk. He wants to see me at ten o'clock this morning about one of my cases." He looked at Susannah and smiled. "Not yours. Don't worry."

She pretended to wipe sweat off her forehead. "Thank goodness."

"So you can't drive me to my appointment in Casper

at eleven." Wyatt considered the other options. "Garrett's got office hours at the church today."

"Which leaves Dylan and Caroline to handle rodeo practice for the kids."

"No problem." The solution was simple. "I'll drive myself." After months of depending on other people to take him places, he relished the prospect of getting out on his own.

Ford made a slicing motion with his hand. "Not till you get the okay from the doctor, you won't."

"I'm able to drive," Wyatt said. "I'll make sure I wear the brace."

"It's not worth the liability if something happened," the lawyer pointed out. "Driving impaired is a lawsuit waiting to happen."

Wyatt glared at him. "I am not impaired."

"I can drive you," Susannah said from the sink. "I'll be glad to."

Before he could react, Ford clapped his hands together. "Great idea. That solves the problem. Thanks, Susannah." In another moment, he was gone.

Finishing his breakfast, Wyatt tried to invent a good reason for leaving Susannah at home. Unfortunately, only the truth occurred to him. He'd been staying out of the house or in his room as much as possible because spending time with Susannah only made him want *more*—more of her company, more connection, more commitment. Even though he had no right to ask.

And no right to tell her how he felt.

Which left him without an excuse for avoiding her offer to help.

So he found himself in the passenger seat of his own truck with Amber in the back seat and Susannah at the wheel. Turning onto the county road, she glanced in his direction.

"You're grumpy," she said. "You don't like being driven."

"Not hardly," he admitted. "How did you know?"

She gave one of her deep, rich chuckles. "You get a wrinkle between your eyebrows when you're aggravated about something. And your mouth goes straight."

"And here I thought I was being stoic." He tried not to picture what his face might be doing. "Doesn't mean I don't appreciate your time. I'm just tired of being…"

"Babied? I would imagine so. You're the caretaker, not used to being taken care of. And you've done a great job," she said as they accelerated onto the interstate highway. "Ford and Garrett and Dylan are wonderful. I know you're proud of them."

"Sure. When they aren't being pains in the butt." Like Ford, today.

"Well, of course. But your parents must have been great examples for you to follow." When he didn't say anything, she glanced over. "There's that wrinkle again. What's wrong?"

He ignored the temptation to change the subject, though they were heading into dangerous territory. "My mom was sick a lot, as I told you. She was sweet and loving but not very strong."

"Which might be why you hate depending on your brothers."

"Ouch."

"Just a thought."

"My dad…" Deep breath. "He adored her. Lived for her. And he fell apart when she died. Started drinking on the night we buried her. And never stopped."

Susannah reached across the console and set her hand over his where it rested on his thigh. "I'm so sorry."

Wyatt didn't move. Barely breathed. Her simple touch seemed to be such a monumental gift that he wasn't sure what to do, how to respond.

After a few moments, her hand returned to the steering wheel. "So you lost two parents at the same time."

He didn't mean to sound pitiful. "My brothers weren't hard to handle. We took care of each other."

"Your dad died of his alcoholism?"

"More or less. He was driving drunk and crashed his car." There it was again, that urge to tell Susannah what he'd never confessed to anyone else. "It was my fault."

Her startled gaze flashed across the cab. "I don't believe you."

"We had a fight that night. After Ford and the others were asleep. A real wrestling match with a few punches thrown for good measure. He stormed out, got in the car and…" In silence, Wyatt lifted a hand, let it fall.

"And left you believing you're responsible for the whole family," Susannah said, completing his sentence. "You think you owe your brothers your own life because he died that night."

Wyatt couldn't deny the truth. So he didn't say anything at all. As they rode to the Casper city limits, only the growl of the truck engine and Amber's nonsense singing over her coloring book broke the silence. He spoke up only when he had to give her directions to the doctor's office, which Susannah followed without speaking.

In the clinic parking lot, she shut off the engine and then shifted in the seat to face him. "You've never told them what happened. About the fight."

He met her serious, intent blue gaze. "No."

"So you've carried that burden all these years, on your own." She sighed. "You're a stubborn man."

He managed a half smile. "I've heard that before."

"Mommy," Amber piped up, "are we getting out?"

"I am," Wyatt said. "There's a playground just a couple of blocks over—more fun than a waiting room."

Susannah nodded. "We'll come back in an hour—don't worry if you're not finished. We won't leave without you."

But even though he had to endure an X-ray and then wait to talk with the doctor, he walked out of the office in less than sixty minutes, grinning like a fool. When the truck pulled up beside him, he held the hated brace over his head in one hand.

"Where's the nearest trash can?" he asked as Susannah rolled down the window. Then he got a good look at her pale face, her shadowed eyes. "What's wrong?"

"Travis," she said in a strangled voice. "At the playground."

He threw the brace in the bed of the truck and leaned in the window. "Did he hurt you? Is Amber okay?"

"We're fine. It's just the shock. He said he followed us from the ranch. He said you h-had so much land, it was easy to watch without b-being seen."

Wyatt glanced around the parking lot and the street alongside it but didn't find the beat-up blue truck Bradley drove. "What did he want?"

"To talk to Amber." Susannah squeezed her eyes shut for a few seconds. "I was sitting on a bench while she played on the slide. As soon as she saw him, she ran to me and buried her face in my lap." Her shoulders lifted on a deep, shaking breath. "He kept coaxing her to look at him. Promising treats and toys. But she wouldn't."

"Did he get mad?"

She nodded. "He started yelling at us, but the other mothers noticed. So he stomped off. I didn't see where he went."

Her hands gripped the frame of the window. Wyatt put his palms over them and found her fingers clammy and cold. With a deep breath, he tamped down on his anger, making sure he stayed calm and quiet. "Everything is okay. He won't bother you again. This time we will tell Ford—Travis can't keep violating that protection order."

Opening the truck door, he offered a hand to help her down and then walked her around to the passenger seat. "Just relax," he said as she settled in. "You and Amber are safe with me."

He looked in on the little girl as he came back to the driver's side. "You okay, Princess?"

Eyes wide, face solemn, she nodded. The absence of her usual saucy grin riled him almost as much as her mother's distress.

As he drove the truck toward the interstate, Susannah put a hand on his arm. "Weren't you going to pick up your computer at the repair shop while we were down here?"

He shrugged. "Not a big deal. I'll come another day."

"But it makes sense to do that now. Why waste the fuel?"

Wyatt couldn't argue with her logic. "Okay. It won't take but a couple of minutes." He parked right in front of the shop window and locked the truck doors while he was inside. Bradley would not get to them again. Ever.

Mission accomplished, they headed north. He kept an eye on the rearview mirror, scanning for Bradley's vehicle, without success.

After a few minutes, Susannah seemed to finally

relax. She turned sideways, her knees drawn up on the seat. "On a more cheerful note, I take it you're free? No more brace?"

"Free and clear." He bent forward over the steering wheel and then sat up straight again, just because he could.

"The doctor had nothing to say about what you should or shouldn't do now? You're back to 'full speed ahead'?"

"No bucking broncs," he said with a grin. "No steer wrestling. No lifting over a hundred pounds for a couple of months. Basically he told me to use common sense."

"That's what has me worried," she teased. "I gather you're planning to ride again. Soon."

"This afternoon, I'm thinking. Caesar has been eating himself silly in the pasture all summer. It's time he got to work. It's time *I* got back to work, took some of the load off Ford and Dylan and Garrett. They've got their own jobs to do. I should do mine."

"Law, art and ministry," she said, slowly. "They're cowboys because you went to work on the ranch as a teenager. Then they all left to follow their dreams. But you stayed, all these years, holding the ranch and the family together. I have to wonder what your goals once were. What you wanted to do."

When he glanced at her, he found her blue gaze intense.

"What did *you* dream about, Wyatt, before your world caved in?"

Chapter Six

He was silent so long Susannah began to wonder if she'd offended him by asking.

"History," he said, at last. "Even as a kid, I loved reading books about the past." A slight smile lifted his mouth. "Especially ancient battles."

"Where would that have taken you?"

This pause wasn't quite so long. "My mom and I talked about college. I thought I might teach one day. Maybe write books." He shook his head. "As you said, just dreams."

"Though not forgotten. You still read history."

"When I have a chance. Just for fun."

A possibility occurred to her. "Have you considered going to college?"

He snorted a laugh. "Not in over twenty years."

"The world needs good teachers." Watching him with Amber, she was sure he would be.

"The Circle M needs a full-time manager."

But what did *he* need? "Is that what you really want to do? Your brothers have their own lives now—you're not a caretaker anymore. Maybe this is the point to reconsider your goals. Your future."

His frown should have warned her. "The ranch is my past, my present and my future. That's all there is to it."

"But are you happy?"

He blew out an exasperated breath. "I promised Henry MacPherson I'd take care of his land and his cattle for the rest of my life. I intend to honor that promise. Maybe it's not what I thought I wanted when I was a kid—hell, there are plenty of days in the year I'd rather be a history teacher or a short-order cook at Kate's Diner, anything besides going out in a cold, windy rain to take care of cattle too dumb to stay safe on their own. But that's what I do because that's the job.

"Whether I'm happy or not doesn't matter one damn bit."

Susannah sat back against her seat. "I…see." What else had she expected? He was obviously a man for whom commitment mattered most of all. "Mr. MacPherson would be proud."

"I hope so."

Knowing what had happened to Wyatt when he was just a teenager, she understood his dedication to the ranch and to his brothers. Her years with Travis had sown in her an equal dedication to her children, a determination to build for them a life free of worry and of the threat of looming catastrophe. She'd brought them into this world. They would always come first. But in the last few months, she'd realized that what she wanted mattered, too. That she had to grow as a person.

After a mostly silent ride to the ranch, Susannah walked around the front of the truck as Wyatt helped Amber out of the backseat. "Give me about ten minutes," she said in an effort at a truce, "and I'll have some sandwiches made for lunch."

"Don't worry about me." He looked up the hill toward the barn. "I think I'll go pull that horse of mine in and give him a good brushing. Then we'll go out for a walk." Though he faced her, his eyes didn't quite meet hers. "Thanks, anyway. With the good breakfast you made this morning, I'm not likely to starve."

Amber, who hadn't said a word since the playground, raised her head. "Can I see your horse?"

"Another time—" Susannah started.

But Wyatt crouched down to Amber's level. "You want to meet Caesar?" When she nodded, he did, too. "Then let's go get him." He straightened up and held out his hand. "Come on."

Susannah followed, watching with a smile as her daughter hopped and skipped alongside the big man in a display of the perfect trust a child should have in her father.

If this were a perfect world.

But the world wasn't perfect. *Or at least I'm not,* Susannah thought. She'd made the mistake of running away with Travis, an emotional choice that had turned out badly for herself and her children. Surely, with all that had happened, she'd learned her lesson. Surely, she could use reason and logic to move her life in the right direction.

Inside the barn, Wyatt led Amber into the tack room for a moment and then through the double doors and out into the corral where the kids had often practiced their riding. They crossed to the gate on the far side, where Susannah joined them to gaze out over the wide, rolling pasture beyond. Only a few horses grazed the tall grass—the kids had taken their animals out for a trail ride this afternoon. In the distance loomed the Bighorn Mountains, sharp peaks in shades of purple and green, accented by puffy white clouds being chased by the wind across a wide, bright blue sky.

"Beautiful," Susannah breathed. "Such a magnificent landscape."

"It is." Wyatt pulled in a deep breath. "I'm privileged to work and live here."

She understood his point. Before she could say so, he put two fingers in his mouth and produced a long, sharp, three-note whistle.

"Ooh," Amber said. "Do it again."

Wyatt obliged. A horse trumpeted from far away, and then from closer, and closer still. The horses nearby startled and began to run across the field, their hooves drumming on the earth.

Amber jumped up and down. "Is he coming? Is it Caesar?"

"He's on his way," Wyatt said. "Watch, now."

In another moment, a horse charged over the horizon, gleaming silver in the sunlight. Ignoring the other animals galloping around the field, he headed straight for the gate at full speed. Susannah grabbed Amber's shoulders to pull her out of the way. She didn't see how the horse could possibly stop in time.

He swerved at the last instant, circled and returned to prance in place in front of the gate. Up close, his coat wasn't silver but spotted white on gray, contrasted by his black mane and tail. Head held high on a proudly arched neck, he surveyed them with expectation in his dark eyes.

"Yeah, I know what you want." Wyatt reached into the pocket of his jeans and brought out sugar cubes. "Big baby." He flattened his hand and reached through the gate so Caesar's mobile lips could suck the treat into his mouth.

The inevitable happened next. "Can I feed him?" Amber asked. "Can I?"

"Hold your hand just like this." Wyatt demonstrated and Amber followed suit. "Now I'll put the sugar on your palm. Just reach out…right…leave your fingers flat…"

Susannah held her breath, but Amber followed directions, allowing Caesar to take sugar without biting her. "It tickles!" She giggled. "Can I do it again?"

Wyatt took the halter off his shoulder. "Let's get him inside and brushed first. Don't want to spoil him too much."

Susannah expected the horse to resist being caught after months off work. But Caesar calmly put his head down and allowed the red halter to slip into place, and then he followed quietly as he was led to the barn.

Watching Wyatt brush the horse, she was struck by the closeness between man and animal. "You have a real relationship, don't you? You're not just… I don't know… just using him. And Caesar understands that."

"I like to think so. I depend on him when we're working, so I take care of him the best I can." He glanced down at Amber, who was brushing the horse's dark legs. "How's it going, Princess?"

"Good. His knees are really dirty."

Susannah noticed the streaks of grime on her daughter's face and grinned. "So are you now." With grooming, Caesar's beautiful mottling had become even more obvious. "What do you call his coat color?"

"He's a dappled gray." Wyatt pulled a comb through the black mane. "He'll bleach out as he gets older and might be pure white one day. Or he could stay dappled. We'll have to wait and see."

"That would be beautiful, too."

The saddle Wyatt brought from the tack room was dark mahogany leather, well-used but not worn. A red saddle blanket went underneath.

"Can I sit on him?" Amber asked. "Can I ride him?"

He scooped her up and set her in the saddle. "How's that?"

"I'm so high!" She picked up the reins, which were lying on the horse's neck. "Let's go, Caesar!"

Susannah was glad they were still in the stall and couldn't actually walk off. "I don't believe horses are in our future," she told Wyatt. "You probably shouldn't encourage her."

"They will be if Nate has anything to say about it. Have you watched him on a horse?"

"Yes, but I doubt the next place we live will be anything like your ranch. In fact…" She blew out a breath. "I probably should start looking for a job and a new place to live. It would be good to be settled before the kids start school."

"There's no reason to hurry." His back was to her as he lifted Amber down. "You're welcome to stay as long as you want to."

She tried to make a joke of it. "Now that your life will be returning to normal, you won't be needing me anymore."

He straightened up, and their eyes met. "I don't think that's true."

His words were polite. But his expression—intense, questioning, somehow wistful—meant more than just manners. What did he want that she could give?

Then Caesar snorted and stamped his foot. Wyatt moved away. "Tired of standing there, son? Let's take a walk."

Out in front of the barn, Susannah kept Amber off to the side while Wyatt checked the fit of the saddle and the cinch. "Yeah, you're two holes bigger than last

spring—eating too much and not exercising enough."
He winked at her. "Just like me."

But for a man who hadn't been riding, he mounted
with amazing ease—his left foot went into the stirrup
and then a smooth swing of the other leg up and across
put him on the saddle. He shifted his hips, settling in,
and looked down at them. "I will join you ladies for supper. Have a good afternoon."

Susannah could only nod—she found herself speechless at the sight of Wyatt seated on his favorite horse.
His broad shoulders and flat waist, his tight butt and the
pull of denim across the strong muscles of his thighs, the
easy curl of his fingers around the reins—all revealed
an aspect of him she hadn't been aware of, a physical
authority she couldn't help responding to.

She'd loved Wyatt for weeks now with her heart and
her mind and her soul.

Suddenly, she wanted him with a fierce desire she
hadn't experienced since she was a teenager.

As he rode away from them, Amber pulled on her
skirt. "Mommy, can we have lunch? I'm hungry."

"Me, too," Susannah said. But her gaze hadn't strayed
from the vanishing cowboy. *Me, too.*

NATE WAS ON the cleanup team after lunch, so Becky
waited until he'd finished to talk to him about the dance.
She could tell he was reluctant to join her by the way
he dried the dishes as slowly as humanly possible. Doo-
dling in her notebook, she just smiled and waited for
him to give in.

Finally, he sat down across the table from her. "What
is it we're doing here?"

"Well, first we need a theme. For the dance."

"Isn't dancing a theme? As opposed to… I don't know…football?"

Boys were dumb. "You have to pick an idea to organize everything else around—decorations, food, clothes. You know, like for a fiesta, you would do Mexican food, have a piñata, wear sombreros."

Nate nodded. "That sounds good. Do that."

"Everybody does that. We should have something different." She was beginning to understand Lizzie's point of view.

"I got it." He slapped the table. "We could do a Western theme. We'd all wear jeans and boots. Especially since they're pretty much the only clothes we have."

She didn't want to shut him down. "It's an idea. Keep thinking."

But he got mad anyway. "What is the big deal? It's just a couple of hours on a Friday night with some music."

"It's our last night at camp. Don't you want to make it special?"

"Oh, yeah." A funny expression came over his face, part surprise, part worry. "I hadn't thought about it like that."

"And since Lizzie and Lena refused to help, I want to do something that everybody will think is awesome."

"Awesome is hard to pull off." His resistance seemed to have melted. "You could have everybody dress as the horse they've been riding. I'll wear blue and you could wear a chestnut color."

"And we'd eat hay and oatmeal?" She grinned at him and was thrilled to get a smile in return.

"Carrot sticks and oatmeal cookies—my mom makes great ones. We could have an apple-bobbing contest. See who can pick it up with their teeth out of a tub of water."

"That's kind of crazy. But it could be fun. What do you think Marcos and Thomas would say?"

Out of nowhere, Lizzie appeared on Nate's side of the table. "About what?" Without being invited—and definitely not wanted—she pulled out a chair and sat down. "What are you two doing?"

"Planning the dance," Nate told her. "Becky said you weren't helping."

"Well, I didn't know there was a meeting. I'm always interested in dancing." She gave him a wink.

Becky groaned silently. Her big chance was gone.

"So what are you planning?" Lizzie propped her arms on the table. "The fiesta idea or the hoedown theme? I thought they were both pretty boring."

Nate explained his idea. "But I was just kidding. It's a dumb idea."

"No, it's not," Becky protested before Lizzie could say something mean. "It's different. I like it."

The glance Lizzie sent her way pretty much declared war. Then she smiled sweetly at Nate. "I think it's a good idea. Different from the usual stuff. We can use hay bales around the dance floor as tables or to sit on. I'm not sure about the apple bobbing, though. It would mess up my hair."

"Maybe only the boys will do that," Nate said. "And the winner gets a prize."

"Good idea!" Lizzie put her hand on his arm. "What kind of prize? Wait, I know…a kiss from the girl of their choice!"

Nate's face flushed red. "Uh, could be, I guess."

"I can't see the grown-ups going for that," Becky said. "They're always pulling Lena and Justino apart."

"We won't tell them. It'll be a secret for just the kids.

That makes it even more fun." She clapped her hands. "This will be great."

Marcos came over from the couch. "What's going on?"

"We're planning the dance," Lizzie said. "And we're having a contest with a secret prize."

"Yeah?" He sat down beside Becky. "What's the prize?"

In another minute, Thomas had joined them. He and Marcos both approved of the apple-bobbing idea. With Lizzie, they started tossing around wild ideas for decorations and music. Nate, of course, had gone silent. He never tried to compete with the other boys.

Becky closed her notebook. So much for getting him to notice her.

Lizzie looked her way. "Why don't you talk to Ms. Susannah about the food? The boys and I will work on the decorations." She managed to include the three of them in her flirty smile. "You three are strong, so I'll need you to move the hay bales."

"Right." Becky understood she'd been dismissed, so she stood up and pushed her chair in. She mouthed *thanks* in Nate's direction. But his eyes were on Lizzie.

Outside the bunkhouse, the bright sun made her squint, which sent tears dripping onto her cheeks. She wiped them off quickly. If he could be fooled by Lizzie, Nate wasn't worth crying over. There would be a guy someday who wanted more than just makeup and smooth blond curls. Who didn't mind red hair. Or freckles. Who would defend her instead of abandoning her.

Like Mr. Ford, who'd left a big job in California to be with Ms. Caroline in Wyoming. Because she mattered more to him than anything else in the world.

Behind her, the door opened and the four of them

FREE Merchandise and a Cash Reward† are 'in the Cards' for you!

Dear Reader,

We're giving away FREE MERCHANDISE and a CASH REWARD!

Seriously, we'd like to reward you for reading this novel by giving you **FREE MERCHANDISE** worth over **$20** retail plus a CASH REWARD! And no purchase is necessary!

You see the Jack of Hearts sticker above? Paste that sticker in the box on the Free Merchandise Voucher inside. Return the Voucher today… and we'll send you Free Merchandise plus a Cash Reward!

Thanks again for reading one of our novels—and enjoy your Free Merchandise and Cash Reward with our compliments!

Pam Powers
Pam Powers

P.S. Look inside to see what Free Merchandise is **"in the cards"** for you!

We'd like to send you two free books like the one you are enjoying now. Your two books have a combined price of over $10 retail, but they are yours to keep absolutely FREE! We'll even send you 2 wonderful surprise gifts and a Cash Reward†. You can't lose!

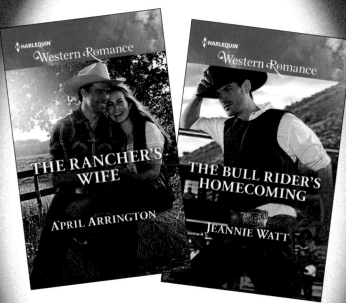

THE RANCHER'S WIFE
APRIL ARRINGTON

THE BULL RIDER'S HOMECOMING
JEANNIE WATT

REMEMBER: Your Free Merchandise, consisting of **2 Free Books** and **2 Free Gifts**, is worth over **$20** retail! Plus we'll send you a **Cash Reward** (it's a dollar) which is really the icing on the cake because it's in addition to your FREE Merchandise! No purchase is necessary, so please send for your Free Merchandise today.

Get TWO FREE GIFTS!
We'll also send you 2 wonderful FREE GIFTS (worth about $10 retail), in addition to your 2 Free books and Cash Reward!

Visit us at:
www.ReaderService.com

Books received may not be as shown.

Detach card and mail today. No stamp needed. ▶

▶

© 2016 HARLEQUIN ENTERPRISES LIMITED. ® and ™ are trademarks owned and used by the trademark owner and/or its licensee. Printed in the U.S.A.

FREE MERCHANDISE VOUCHER

2 FREE
BOOKS
and
2 FREE
GIFTS

Please send my Free Merchandise, consisting of
2 Free Books and **2 Free Mystery Gifts** PLUS my
Cash Reward. I understand that I am under no
obligation to buy anything, as explained
on the back of this card.

154/354 HDL GLTA

Please Print

FIRST NAME

LAST NAME

ADDRESS

APT.#   CITY

STATE/PROV.   ZIP/POSTAL CODE

Offer limited to one per household and not applicable to series that subscriber is currently receiving.
Your Privacy—The Reader Service is committed to protecting your privacy. Our Privacy Policy is available
online at www.ReaderService.com or upon request from the Reader Service. We make a portion of our mailing
list available to reputable third parties that offer products we believe may interest you. If you prefer that we not
exchange your name with third parties, or if you wish to clarify or modify your communication preferences, please
visit us at www.ReaderService.com/consumerschoice or write to us at Reader Service Preference Service, P.O. Box
9062, Buffalo, NY 14240-9062. Include your complete name and address.

NO PURCHASE NECESSARY!

WR-N16-FMC15

▲ If offer card is missing write to: Reader Service, P.O. Box 1867, Buffalo, NY 14240-1867 or visit www.ReaderService.com ▲

BUSINESS REPLY MAIL
FIRST-CLASS MAIL   PERMIT NO. 717   BUFFALO, NY

POSTAGE WILL BE PAID BY ADDRESSEE

READER SERVICE
PO BOX 1867
BUFFALO NY 14240-9952

NO POSTAGE
NECESSARY
IF MAILED
IN THE
UNITED STATES

came through, laughing, the three boys clustered around Lizzie like bees on a daisy.

Becky sighed and headed for the barn. *Or maybe not.*

FORD CAME INTO the barn as Wyatt was unsaddling Caesar. "I take it your doctor's appointment went well?"

"I'm cleared for duty, more or less." He carried the saddle into the tack room with Ford following. "Though I won't be lifting any hundred-pound bales for a while yet." He set the saddle on its rack, pulled a soft cloth out of the nearby bucket and began to wipe off the leather. "But we've got a problem. Travis Bradley accosted Susannah and Amber in Casper today."

"An unlikely coincidence."

"It is. Evidently he's been on the property. He told her we've got plenty of land and it's easy to watch us without being seen."

The attorney's list of swear words was long and colorful. "Did you call the sheriff?"

"I wanted to let you know first. I didn't catch him following us. Susannah and Amber were both shaken up, so we just came back here."

"At least you told me this time." Ford's voice was dangerously smooth.

Wyatt acknowledged his mistake with a nod. "She was afraid he'd get more worked up, do something worse. It was her choice, so I went along with it." Which, in hindsight, had been a bad idea.

Ford confirmed that opinion. "Not your best thinking, Boss. He could have been in jail by now instead of lurking around, waiting to pounce on her again." Those blue eyes, so like their dad's, were stern. "I'm her attorney. I need to know when things happen. Makes me wonder what other secrets you've been keeping."

I killed him, Wyatt thought. *If it weren't for me he would have stayed home and passed out in his bed. I'm the reason he died.* He hadn't been able to face that confession when he was sixteen, and he couldn't now.

"I'll get hold of Deputy Wade Daughtrey," Ford said, again heading for the tack room door. "Maybe he can have Bradley locked up before bedtime. Assuming they can find him."

The bad news came in late that night after all the kids had gone to bed—Travis Bradley could not be located. No one at his regular bar had seen him for weeks. He'd always been a loner, so there were few friends to question and none of them knew where he was. The trailer Susannah had lived in showed no sign of being occupied in recent days.

"He's out there somewhere," Wyatt said, when Ford had left the house to walk Caroline up to the girls' cabin. "And we can't do a thing about it." He rubbed a hand over his face. "I should have hauled him in when I had the chance."

"This is my fault." Susannah stood beside the fireplace with her arms wrapped around her waist. "I convinced you not to call the sheriff. Instead of appeasing Travis, I've only made the situation worse. I ought to have trusted Ford." She looked at Wyatt. "I ought to have trusted you."

"You were protecting your kids." He wanted to put his arms around her, to make her feel safe. But he stayed where he was across the room. "Maybe you ought to get some rest. It's been a long day."

"You could be right." She straightened her shoulders and gave him a smile. "There's something comforting about watching children sleep. They relax like there can't be anything wrong in the world."

He left a lamp on for Ford and then followed her as she started down the hallway. "I guess we lose that trust when we realize the world isn't always going to take care of us."

"Which you found out at an early age." She stopped at her door and took hold of the knob, but she rested her head against the panel instead of opening it. "I wish my children hadn't learned it so soon." Despair wavered in her voice.

"Susannah." Wyatt closed his hands over her shoulders, massaging gently the tense muscles under his fingers. "It'll be alright. You'll get through this. I'll make sure of it."

She sighed. "That feels good." More softly, she said, "Your hands are so big and strong."

His body tightened at the husky words, but only a deep breath betrayed him. When she tilted her head from side to side, he moved his grip to the cords between her shoulders and neck, still kneading at the stiffness.

"Wonderful," she whispered. After a few moments, she turned around to face him. Her palms came to rest on his ribs. In the dim light of the hall, she gazed up at him, her eyes wide and dark. "You're wonderful."

Before he could shake his head, she raised up on her tiptoes and kissed his mouth. Once. And again.

The second time, he kissed her back. Tenderly, unselfishly, he hoped. No demand, no compulsion, just the intent to make her feel how much he cared. How much he loved her.

So it was Susannah who pushed them over the edge. She leaned into him and wrapped her arms around his neck. Her lips urgently sought his, requiring response. He gave her what she asked for—the surge of mouth against mouth, the desperate press and slide of sensitive flesh, a sensuous dance of tongue against tongue. He pulled her tight against his body, fueling the ache she kindled inside him.

Voices and the squeak of the screen door in the living room brought Wyatt to his senses. He lifted his head, breathing hard.

Susannah gave a choked sob and let her forehead drop to his chest.

"Shh, shh." He stepped back, bringing his hands to her shoulders. "Go in your room now. Go on."

She disappeared behind the door, and Wyatt waited until he heard his brothers cross into the kitchen. He scrubbed his hands over his face, took a deep breath and blew it out. Then he went down the hall to the kitchen door.

They hadn't turned on many lights, which was good for him. "What's going on?"

Garrett stood peering into the refrigerator. "I didn't get anything to eat at the hospital tonight, so I'm foraging for leftovers." He'd spent the evening with the family of a sick church member.

Wyatt sat down at the table. "How's Mr. Davis?"

"Still in the intensive care unit but improving slightly." Garrett brought an armful of containers to the breakfast bar. "A chicken sandwich sounds about perfect. Especially with some of the vegetables Susannah roasts in the same pan."

"How about making two of those?" Ford said. "I wouldn't mind a late-night snack. Dinner was a long time ago."

"Heck, I can make three. Want one, Wyatt?"

"I'll pass." The last thing he needed was food. His system was still stirred up over Susannah—his pulse drumming, his skin tingling. He couldn't believe his brothers hadn't noticed. If they had, they surely would have said something.

Instead, Ford filled Garrett in on the situation with Travis Bradley. "Jail would have been a good solution," Garrett said as he brought plates and glasses of milk to the table. "Can the divorce proceed without him?"

"An excellent question." Ford took a bite, chewed and swallowed. "I'll work on the answer tomorrow. In the meantime, we have the junior rodeo coming up in just two weeks. Can we get Lena, Marcos and Thomas on livestock again before they compete?"

"Seems like a good idea." Wyatt welcomed the shift of subject away from Susannah. "They can use all the preparation we provide. I'll call Dave Hicks in the morning, ask if we can use his arena and a few steers." They had spent a day at Hicks's Twin Oaks Ranch in July, giving the three kids who wanted to ride rough stock a chance to practice on young animals.

Garrett finished his own food and half of Ford's. "I'll ask Rachel if she can spend the day with us. I like having her as medical backup."

Sitting on his other side, Ford punched him lightly in the arm. "You just like having Rachel around, period."

Their brother's grin brightened the room. "I'm not denying that." After a rocky start, Garrett and the new doctor in town had forged a strong relationship and they'd recently become engaged to be married. "In fact, I'm expecting her to call any minute." Moving briskly, he cleared away the dishes and returned the food to the fridge. "So I'll see you two in the morning." Almost as soon as his door closed, the phone rang. Once.

Ford chuckled. "Every day is Valentine's Day for Garrett in love. Pretty entertaining."

"And you're so jaded?" Wyatt shook his head. "You

should see the way your face lights up when Caroline comes into the room."

"Yes, well..." His expression softened into his own version of a lover's smile. "She's a special woman." Then he blew out a breath. "Too bad about Dylan, though. He's missing Jess more than I realized he would."

"Healing from a breakup takes awhile."

"Right." As Wyatt stood up, though, Ford raised a hand. "You and I have to talk. About Susannah."

"There's nothing to talk about." He remained on his feet.

Ford stood, as well. "You're getting involved with her. It was written all over your face when you came into the kitchen."

So much for discretion. "It's none of your concern."

"You're my brother. I don't want you to get hurt."

"Not a problem."

"She's not in a place to take on a new relationship, Wyatt. That bastard Bradley keeps her off balance."

"I understand that." He could barely force the words through his teeth.

"Caroline and I have talked about this. Susannah's been married to him since she was a teenager. Assuming everything goes well and she gets a divorce fairly soon, she's going to need time on her own, space to figure out what she wants to do with her life. I hate to say this, but that may or may not include you."

Wyatt managed not to flinch.

"And Bradley is not going to vanish. Those are his kids, and he will be entitled to visitation, if not shared custody. Should you and Susannah share a life, he will be part of it for the next ten to fifteen years. I know that wouldn't change your feelings for her, but you ought to consider what you're looking forward to. A relationship with Susannah means inviting complications you can't begin to foresee."

"I'm aware. And you're way out of line."

"Then I'll step a little further." He put a hand on Wyatt's arm. "A woman in Susannah's situation is vulnerable. Not necessarily thinking straight—or she would have reported Bradley being here the first time and solved most of the problem. So you ought to ask yourself whether her emotions at this point are really what you're hoping they are. You've given her a refuge and a job, taken care of her children this summer. What you're interpreting as love might, in fact, be gratitude."

Without waiting for a response, Ford pressed on. "Are you prepared for her to realize one day that you're not the man she wants to spend the rest of her life with? Or have her stay with you out of a sense of obligation?"

Hands clenched into fists, Wyatt didn't move.

Darkness boiled inside of him. He wanted to rage against the facts, pummel the idea that he and Susannah weren't meant to be together, even if that included battering the brother who said so.

But part of him remained sane enough to walk away. He couldn't form words, but he could turn, stride down the hallway and across the living room, out the front door. He jolted down the porch steps and headed up the hill. Behind him, Honey whined at the screen door, wanting to come along. Wyatt didn't go back.

At the corral gate, he whistled for Caesar. The gelding trotted over, looking sleepy and a little puzzled to be called in the middle of the night. After a quick and dirty brush down—just the area under the blanket—Wyatt tacked up and led the horse outside. As he settled into the saddle, he heard Ford call his name.

Nope.

Urging Caesar into a jog, he headed away from the house and the barn, away from the pain and out onto the land he tended, the fields he cared for, under the cloudless, star-flecked sky and the brilliant light of a full Wyoming moon.

Chapter Seven

"Wake up, Mommy. It's breakfast time."

With a gasp, Susannah sat bolt upright in bed. Amber always slept till seven. That would mean...

She swallowed the words that came to mind—she wouldn't swear in front of her daughter. "Thanks, sweetie. I overslept, didn't I?"

"Why did you?"

"I, um, don't know." She recalled lying in bed thinking about Wyatt's hot kisses, his arms firm and secure around her, his hair soft and thick against her fingers. Last night, he'd made her feel cherished, valued. Most of all, desirable.

And now he'd been waiting for his breakfast for probably an hour. Anxious to see him, to share a smile or even a brief—but knowing—look, she skipped her shower, changed clothes and twisted her hair up in about five minutes, deciding not to waste time on makeup.

Then she took Amber's hand. "Okay, let's go cook some breakfast!"

In the kitchen, three cowboys stood around the breakfast bar, coffee mugs in hand. They all stared at her as she and Amber came through the door.

"I'm so sorry," Susannah said right away. "I don't understand what happened."

"Mommy slept too much," Amber explained.

Garrett laughed. Dylan raised his mug in a salute. "You deserve it, hard as you work around here."

Wyatt took a long drink of coffee. He didn't so much as smile.

"I'll get breakfast started." She hurried to the refrigerator to bring out eggs, bacon and butter. "Biscuits would take too long, but I baked some bread earlier in the week. I'll make toast."

"Sounds great," Garrett said. "Don't rush. Nobody here's going to starve."

Something about Wyatt's silence pressured her. "There are potatoes in the freezer, so I can get some hash browns going…" She pulled out the bag but dropped it on the floor. "Dammit," she said, bending to pick it up.

Amber gasped. "Mommy said a bad word."

"Tell you what," Dylan said to Amber, "why don't you and I go into the living room and play horsey while your mom cooks? Sound like fun?"

"Yay!" Holding his hand, she led him through the dining room door.

Back at the counter with the potatoes, Susannah found her hands shaking as she used a knife to open the package. Garrett came to stand beside her and took the knife out of her hand. "Let me." He slit the bag and then handed it back to her. "Are you okay?"

"Of course." She was all too aware of Wyatt, who stood staring down into his mug.

"I forgot to tell Rachel something last night," Garrett said as if he'd suddenly remembered. "I'd better call her. See you in a few minutes."

Wyatt looked up to frown at him. "*That's* not obvious."

His brother shrugged. "You two need to talk. That

is what's obvious. Call me when it's time to eat." In another moment, the door to his room closed with a thud.

"We don't have to talk," Susannah said. "I'll just get breakfast ready—"

"No, we do." Wyatt crossed to the coffeemaker and refilled his cup. "About last night."

"Don't apologize," she said vehemently. "I'm not sorry. I'm not."

"I'm not, either." He gave her a slight smile. "But we can't. I've thought about it all night. That's not what you need."

With a glance, Susannah realized he was wearing the same shirt and jeans he'd had on yesterday. Had he not been to bed at all?

Then she processed his words. "What I need?" She turned to face him. "I don't understand."

"Your life has fallen apart. You're confused, uncertain, weary."

Not a flattering picture. "It's been hard," she admitted.

"You're grateful for the help you've gotten this summer, grateful for the protection, a place to stay, a job."

"You think I kissed you because I'm grateful?" Her temper spiked. "And why did you kiss me? Because I owe you?"

"No!" He avoided her gaze. "But we've been together a lot this summer. Maybe too much. You should take some time and space to get your life together, figure out where you're going. You might decide that what you want for yourself and your kids is somewhere else. With someone else. And I… I don't want to get involved with another woman who plans to leave."

Another woman. The words seared her heart. "So this is about you trying to protect yourself?"

Now he glared at her. "This is about me trying to do what's best for both of us."

"Thanks so much." Susannah couldn't remember ever being quite so angry—too angry to find words that would make sense or even to understand what was making her so mad. Hadn't she thought exactly the same thing herself? "Then I had better get back to doing *my job*." Deciding the eggs would be scrambled this morning, she fetched a bowl and began cracking shells on the rim, not caring for once if a little of the whites dripped onto the counter. Whisk in hand, she discovered that beating up yolks made a satisfying substitute for arguing with a stubborn, obtuse man.

Wyatt stood where he was for a few moments, as if he couldn't think of anything else to do. She ignored him, pretending to concentrate on her cooking, until he moved across the kitchen and sat at the breakfast bar. The distance between them didn't lessen her disappointment, her distress over his conclusions. After last night, she'd expected something very different from this new day.

Except...wasn't that the same kind of impulsive reaction that got her involved with Travis in the first place?

With bread in the toaster, she called Dylan, Amber and Garrett to the kitchen. Amber sat at the bar between Garrett and Dylan, chattering between bites with her usual energy, keeping the two brothers laughing. Wyatt ate in solemn silence. Susannah couldn't force down a bite and cleaned up the kitchen, instead.

"By the way, Susannah," Garrett said, during a silence while Amber drank some juice, "I heard Kate at the diner wants to hire another server. It's not a wonderful job, but it would be a place to start."

She dredged up a smile for him. "Thanks for the suggestion. I—"

"Not a good idea," Wyatt said, his voice stern. "She should get as far away as possible from Bradley, not put herself out in public, in the middle of his sights."

Susannah glared at him. "We shouldn't talk about this right now." But the damage was done.

Amber set her glass down. "Are we going away, Mommy? I don't want to. I like it here."

And how was she supposed to answer that honestly? "Don't worry, sweetie, we aren't going anywhere today."

Her little girl could be hard to divert. Eyes wide and troubled, she said, "I thought we would live with Mr. Wyatt forever."

Dylan tried an intervention. "You're going to grow up and have a house of your own one day. What kind of house will that be? A castle, maybe?"

Shaking her head, Amber stuck her lower lip out. "I want to live on the ranch. With Caesar. And Honey."

Sensing a tantrum in the making, Susannah scooped her daughter off her chair. "It is fun, isn't it? Let's go get you dressed for the day and then we'll take a walk with Honey down to the creek. The kids are practicing their rodeo riding this morning, so we can watch them for a while before lunch. There's lots to do on a ranch, isn't there? We can visit the horses and feed them some carrots, too. They like that, don't they?"

Carrying the child to their room—that is, the room they were borrowing—Susannah managed to avoid a meltdown. She got Amber into clothes and shoes and then took her straight outside, where the wonders of rocks, trees, grass and animals distracted her. Honey ambled contentedly beside them.

Though she loved the ranch, Susannah couldn't find her own peace or distraction there this morning. Garrett's suggestion of a job at the diner, while helpful, only reinforced what Wyatt had said. She'd spent the summer hiding from reality, letting the Marshall brothers protect her and her children while she ignored the problems in her life. When Travis had intruded, she'd allowed Wyatt to deal with him or, as had happened yesterday, just take her away from the situation. Even her progress toward getting her GED had been at Wyatt's suggestion. Instead of taking responsibility for her own life, she'd accepted his directions. And, as he'd pointed out this morning, she was grateful.

Amber interrupted her musings. "Can we swing, Mommy?"

"Sure." They had reached the cabin where the girls were staying. The bench swing on the front porch was one of Amber's favorite places. Susannah followed her daughter up the steps and sat down as Amber clambered onto the seat. "Here we go." It wasn't an exciting ride, but something about the easy motion could make Amber happy for a long time.

As they swung, the door to the cabin opened. The three girls emerged, stomped down the steps and headed single file toward the bunkhouse.

Caroline stepped out a few minutes later. "Well, good morning, you two! I didn't know you were out here. How are you today, Miss Amber?"

"I'm good. We're swinging." She held up the doll she'd insisted on bringing along. "With Russell."

Susannah nodded toward the teenagers. "None of them said hi on their way out. Wrong side of the bed this morning?"

"This week, is more like it," Caroline said, leaning against the porch rail. "Ever since we announced the dance, they've been worse than wet cats with each other, spitting and hissing. Nobody wants to cooperate." She shook her head. "It doesn't help that the boys have suddenly decided girls exist for more reasons than just to annoy them. Becky and Lizzie are at odds over Nate."

"Nathan? And a girl?" She wasn't sure she was comfortable with that idea. He was only thirteen.

"For Lizzie, it's about the power. But Becky really likes him. He, unfortunately, is dazzled by blond hair. Speaking of which—" Caroline raised an eyebrow "—you're looking a little less than your usual perfect self this morning, though only a little. Is everything alright?"

"More or less." Susannah got up and went to stand beside the swing, where she could still push Amber with her hand. "I overslept. And I'm just now realizing that I've spent the summer avoiding my life. I should have been making plans. But I've coasted along, letting other people—" With Wyatt on her mind, she took a deep breath. "Letting other people decide for me."

Caroline's frown was sympathetic. "You needed time to recover. You were living in a difficult situation for a lot of years. Don't shame yourself for getting some emotional and mental rest." Putting an arm around Susannah's shoulders, she gave her an affectionate squeeze. "Now that you're ready, you can figure out what you want to do. Anything I can help with, just let me know."

Touched by her friend's concern, Susannah leaned into the hug, blinking back tears. They stood for a moment in silence.

"Push me, Mommy!" Amber said. "I stopped swinging."

"I'm sorry." Susannah straightened up and went back to her job. "A mother's work is never done."

"Neither is a camp counselor's," Caroline said, laughing. "I'd better check on breakfast and find out if they're all sitting in there sulking. Have a good day!" She pattered down the steps and strode off toward the bunk-house.

This summer at the ranch, Susannah realized, had given her a taste of security, of caring and confidence. But there were only a couple weeks of camp left. The kids were busy practicing to ride in the junior rodeo, when they weren't working on this dance they were all excited about. Then it would be time for school—and time for her family to leave the protection of the Marshall brothers and strike out on their own.

That meant leaving Wyatt—which would break her heart.

But if she wanted to control her life, if she wanted to reconnect with her parents with her head held high, she couldn't continue hiding on the ranch. She needed to be out in the world, making decisions and taking responsibility for what did and did not happen. Her self-respect demanded as much.

And for the sake of her children, she didn't dare fail.

As FAR AS Wyatt was concerned, nothing about the next week was easy. Talking to the deputy sheriff certainly wasn't, when they had to tell him they hadn't reported Bradley's visit to the ranch. The disbelief and resulting disapproval on Daughtrey's face only confirmed Ford's assessment of the situation. And knowing that Bradley was out there, on Wyatt's own land, maybe with a telescope or binoculars trained on Susannah or Nate or Amber, was enough to make him crazy. He wanted to shut the three of them in the house and sit on the porch with his rifle across his knees until Bradley showed up again.

Because Bradley would show up.

Instead, Wyatt found himself trapped inside, as he

had been all summer, keeping watch without actually locking the place down. Ford, Dylan and Garrett had promised that one of them would always keep Nate in sight. With the boy taken care of, Wyatt made himself responsible for Susannah and Amber.

And that was the most difficult aspect of the situation because his relationship with Susannah had gone so wrong. Having held her, having kissed her, he couldn't encounter her without remembering the intensity of that pleasure, without craving another taste, another touch. Even hearing her voice stirred his hunger. And she was always just a room or two away, so he was pretty much always hungry.

He wanted to do what was best for her, give her the opportunity to choose the direction of her life without the pressure of his feelings. But those feelings kept interfering with his intent. Being in the same room tortured him because he wanted to share everything with her— his ideas about the ranch, his thoughts about history, his reactions to Amber or the weather or the state of the world. The little girl would say something funny at dinner and he would cross glances with Susannah— part laughter, part pride, the kind of look parents would share. He realized he thought of Amber as his own, and that was one of the worst moments of all—he was sending his own away.

At least he'd been successful in his call to Dave Hicks, who said the kids were welcome to come ride steers at his place anytime. They settled on the following Thursday, which gave Dr. Rachel a chance to arrange her appointments so she could come along as medical backup. The teenagers could hardly wait for the day to arrive—any trip off the ranch was a big deal for them.

"I take it you're driving your own truck," Dylan said

to Wyatt that morning, as the kids milled around in the yard, ready to go. "Ford and Caroline will take the van. Do we need another vehicle?"

"Not as long as you ride with them. Rachel and Garrett will go with me. Plus Susannah and Amber." He dreaded the trip—more closeness between them without real intimacy.

Dylan groaned. "Are earphones allowed?"

As they settled in for the drive, Wyatt kept his eyes on the road—mostly—and his thoughts to himself. Beyond a somber "Good morning," Susannah said little and sat staring out the side window, which pretty much ensured that their glances wouldn't cross. Rachel filled the silence with a fairy tale for Amber, one she'd evidently invented during a hayride and campfire earlier in the summer. The little girl remembered the story well and was able to supply several details Rachel had forgotten. Or pretended to, anyway.

Considering the tension in the front seat of the truck, reaching their destination came as a real relief.

Located near the Thunder Basin National Grassland, the Twin Oaks Ranch demonstrated a different type of Wyoming terrain from the Circle M. The land was drier because it was farther away from the mountains but, in its own way, it was just as beautiful. Dave Hicks, a big man with red hair and a mustache, met them in front of his gray barn and shook Wyatt's hand as the kids climbed out of the van. "Gettin' ready for the youth rodeo over in Buffalo, is that right? Should be a good show, especially with these fine competitors in the mix." His glance included not just the three kids who would be riding steers but all the teenagers. "Good to see y'all again. Let's get started."

They traipsed after him toward the arena in the distance with Marcos, Thomas and Lena at the head of the group, anxious for their rides. Lizzie kept up with the two boys but stopped them at the pen holding the steers they would be using.

"I can't believe you're going to do this," she said, shaking her head. "They're so big!"

Marcos stared at the animals. "They do look bigger than last time." He swallowed hard. "But, hey, we're better than we were last time. We know what to expect. No problem."

"I call first up." Thomas had already put on his protective vest. "I'm ready for that bad boy."

"You're so brave," Lizzie told him. "I'd be scared to death."

As Wyatt passed the pen, Nate suddenly turned away from the fence and caught up with him. "Could I try?"

Wyatt stared at the boy. "Riding steers? Today?"

"Yes. And at the rodeo. I don't have an event to ride in."

"I don't think so, son. You haven't practiced like the others."

"But I ride Blue better than any of them on their horses. Even Lena. I gallop up and down the hills bareback. And I've practiced going in between those trees on the far side of the pasture. You know, the ones in a straight line with about twenty feet between them? I can stay on bending from side to side like that, without a saddle. How different can it be?"

"Bucking on a steer and bending on a horse are not the same. With the horse, you're in control. Why are you suddenly so crazy to do this?"

Nate's gaze followed Lizzie and the other two boys as they walked toward the arena. "They're not the only ones who can be brave."

Wyatt could appreciate the desire to impress a girl.

He'd been young once. But the idea was absurd. "They're the ones who have trained for this all summer. You're just asking to get injured."

"But at least I'll have tried. That's something." Nate stared up at him with the same appealing blue eyes as his sister. "Please."

One last weapon. "You'll have to ask your mother."

Those eyes narrowed. "That's not fair."

"You know I can't do it any other way. If she says so, I'll let you have a go."

Nate stalked off toward the bleachers on the far side of the arena where the kids who weren't riding sat with Caroline, Amber, Susannah and Rachel. Following, Wyatt admired the boy's guts. At least he was going to ask, even if the outcome was predictable.

Wyatt arrived at the bleachers in time to hear Susannah's answer.

"Absolutely not."

"Mom..."

She shook her head. "You haven't practiced. And even if you had, I wouldn't allow you to ride. It's just too dangerous."

"The other kids—"

"Don't have me for a mother."

"Mr. Ford—"

"Is not my son."

"If you weren't here," Nate argued in desperation, "I would have done it."

Crossing her arms, she stared at him calmly. "Then you're lucky because I'm keeping you from getting hurt."

Her son held her gaze, pleading in silence, but Susannah didn't budge. None of the other kids, seated nearby, made a sound.

After a minute, Nate's shoulders slumped. He looked

down at the ground and then went to sit by himself at the top corner of the stands, as far from his mother and anyone else as he could manage.

"I told him," Wyatt said, when Susannah glanced at him. "But he had to hear it from you."

"Thank you." She gave him a strained smile. "Saying no isn't easy. I hope he'll forgive me someday."

Before Wyatt could answer, she turned away to check on Amber, seated behind her. Her message was loud and clear. *You set the rules. Now leave me alone.*

He found he couldn't leave Nate without some kind of consolation, however, and went over to sit beside the boy on the top bench. "There is an event you're ready for."

A snort was his answer. "Mutton bustin'? With the little kids?"

"Pole bending. If you've been weaving through that tree line, you could compete."

"It's not bull riding."

"It's harder than it seems," Wyatt told him. "It takes control and the kind of skill a cowboy needs for his work." Having made the offer, he walked away. He'd done his best.

But his best, these days, didn't seem to be anywhere near good enough.

BECKY TOOK TWO drinks from the cooler and climbed up to sit beside Nate at the top of the bleachers. She offered him one of the bottles. "Hey."

He shook his head without saying anything.

"Okay." Setting the bottle between them, she opened her own and took a gulp. "Are you alright?"

"No." After a minute, he said, "I'm a loser."

"You're not a loser." She should know.

"Oh, that's right. I have to compete to be a loser, and I can't even do that."

"Why would you want to?"

At that moment, a steer charged through the gate into the arena with Thomas sitting on its back and holding onto the rope with one hand. The animal kicked up its hind legs, reared and spun, jerking Thomas from front to back and then throwing him off to one side. Mr. Dylan and Mr. Garrett rushed in to get the steer's attention while Thomas crawled out of the way. Once on his feet, he staggered a little as he walked out, shaking his head.

A glance at his face told Becky that Nate had watched the ride. "That didn't go well," she commented but didn't get an answer.

Lena rode next and stayed on longer, but she, too, got bucked off before the whistle blew. "Not a success," Becky said. "Seems like she's limping—hope she's not hurt."

Finally, Marcos took his shot, only to fall off just outside the gate.

"Three up, three down." Becky shifted to the bench in front of him, looking directly into Nate's face. "Why would you want to do that? It's stupid."

Even though she was right in front of him, his gaze traveled around her, down and to the side, stopping where Lizzie sat beside Thomas, listening to him complain about the ride.

"Oh. Right." Suddenly, she felt like her face was on fire. "So you can impress *her*. When she doesn't give a damn about you and never will. You know what?" She spun on the seat, put her feet down and stood up so fast she became a little dizzy. "You *are* a loser. Because you won't see the truth, won't see what's right under your nose, won't see what really matters. You're stupid. Plain stupid."

With tears stinging her eyes, she sidestepped her way to the other end of the stands and sat down. She didn't look back at Nate. Right now, she never wanted to see him again.

And she didn't glance up when his mom sat down beside her. "Men can be very dumb," she said. "Also stubborn."

"I don't care." Becky took a swig from her bottle. "I was just trying to be friendly."

"I understand."

"Lizzie's mean to him. And he doesn't even care. Because she's pretty." The real pain leaked out. "And I'm not."

"You're wrong about that. You are very pretty."

Becky shook her head. She didn't have to repeat what was obvious. What she'd been told often enough.

But Ms. Susannah wouldn't quit. "The advantage Lizzie has is that she looks older. Her hair and makeup are styled for a sixteen-year-old. Your pigtails are cute, but they aren't grown-up. Boys at this age are attracted to grown-up."

"My hair won't do anything else. It's too curly."

"Come with me." Ms. Susannah stood. "Come on. My purse is down at the bottom."

A minute later, Becky sat on the end of a bench with Nate's mother standing behind her, combing her hair. "You have a heart-shaped face," she said, her fingers gentle against Becky's head. "Big brown eyes and plump lips. You're gorgeous. Isn't she?" she asked Ms. Caroline and Ms. Rachel, who instantly agreed.

With her cheeks burning, Becky didn't know where

to look. She wasn't used to being the center of attention. Not unless she'd done something wrong.

"Your freckles are part of your charm," Ms. Caroline added. "And I love the deep red of your hair."

"A little foundation and powder will tone those freckles down," Ms. Rachel said. "That's what I do. You should see me when I just wash my face!"

Becky had never before noticed the redheaded doctor's freckles. "Wow. They *are* there."

She nodded. "They are, but I manage them. You can, too."

"There are lots of ways you could braid your hair," Ms. Susannah said as her fingers worked against Becky's head. "This one's pretty simple—just a ponytail braid in back. But it will keep your hair out of your eyes and show off your bone structure."

Ms. Caroline rummaged through her purse. "I've got a compact with a mirror in here somewhere…there it is." She opened the little powder case and patted the puff over Becky's cheeks and forehead, and then she handed it over. "Take a look."

Becky peered into the mirror and gasped. Funny, she almost didn't recognize herself. With her hair pulled off her face, she looked older. And the powder did help with the freckles. Not that she would ever wear as much makeup as Lizzie did. But… "It really does make a difference."

"A good difference," Ms. Susannah said. "And you can do this yourself. Just don't pull your hair too tight— you want some softness. You could tease out a few loose strands around your face, like that. What do you think?"

She grinned at the new version of herself. "Nate should be so lucky."

And the women standing around her laughed.

After Thomas, Marcos and Lena each made a second ride—Thomas and Marcos stayed on till the whistle but Lena didn't—they ate lunch on the bleachers and then went back to the barn, where Mr. Hicks had a surprise for them. Last time, they'd gone for a stagecoach ride around the ranch with a team of four horses. Today, he'd filled a big red wagon full of loose hay, and they got to enjoy an authentic hayride behind a pair of pale gold draft horses called American Creams. With their amber eyes and white manes and tails, the horses were some of the most unusual and beautiful animals Becky had ever seen.

During the ride, she intercepted startled looks from the other kids—like she'd suddenly grown antlers or pointed ears. No one said anything, though Lena gave her the thumbs-up sign. Nate was the only one who didn't seem to notice that she'd changed anything. Probably because he just didn't care.

That realization darkened the sunny afternoon as far as Becky was concerned, and she sulked through the return trip to the Circle M. Having to clean up the kitchen after dinner didn't improve her mood, and having to do it with Nate only made matters worse.

Then, as she was washing the pot used for spaghetti sauce—an icky job—he said, "Your hair looks nice that way."

She swiveled her head and just stared at him.

He shrugged. "I'm stupid, not blind."

"Well…thanks." She wouldn't let him see her smile. But she had to wonder if maybe, just maybe, there was a little hope after all.

ON THE SATURDAY night after the trip to Twin Oaks Ranch, Susannah woke suddenly, without knowing why. She immediately rolled over to check on Amber. In the scant light from the bedside clock, her little girl lay still, breathing evenly, her cheeks and forehead cool. No problem there.

But then a flash of lightning blazed brightly at the window, followed moments later by the growl of thunder. Mystery explained, Susannah sank back against her pillow—the storm must have disturbed her. Rain started hammering the roof, and lightning flared again. She was grateful Amber would sleep through such weather.

Not so lucky herself, she lay for a while enduring the noise and the light show, counting seconds between flash and roll. They seemed to be coming closer together, unfortunately. Getting to sleep again would take some time.

But with the storm at its peak, Susannah decided she couldn't just lie there anymore. She had to be up and ready, though for what she wasn't sure. After making sure Amber slept on, she eased the bedroom door open and stepped out into the dark hallway. Maybe a drink would help her relax.

In the kitchen, the light shone over the sink as usual. Water eased her thirst, while also demonstrating that her fingers were trembling. She opened the dishwasher to put the tumbler inside.

"Everything okay?"

Susannah gasped and dropped the glass, which landed on the top of her foot and rolled off. "Ow!" She glared at Wyatt. "You startled me."

"I'm sorry about that. Are you alright?"

Bending to pick up the glass, she massaged the top of her foot. "Bruised, but I'll live." With the glass placed securely in the dishwasher, she peered at him where he stood across the room in the shadows. "What are you doing up?"

"Storm woke me. I always think about the animals on a night like this."

There he went, disarming her, damn him. "I guess all they can do is stand there and get wet."

"Pretty much. It's the lightning that's the problem." At his words, a bolt sizzled and cracked nearby with an almost simultaneous boom of thunder.

"I hadn't thought—they could get electrocuted, couldn't they?"

"It happens. We'll be checking the herds over the next few days."

"That would be awful."

They stood in an awkward silence for a few moments. He wore a white T-shirt and sweatpants slung low on his hips. The sexy look, combined with his rumpled hair and sleepy eyes, left her struggling for something to say.

"Storms make you nervous?" he asked, finally.

"How did you guess?"

"You're twisting your hands together. Dead give-away."

"Oh." She pressed them against the sides of her thighs. "I was downright scared of storms as a little girl. Amber doesn't seem to have inherited that problem, I'm glad to say. Or Nate."

"I suspect you helped them understand the weather, taught them that they don't have to be afraid."

Susannah shrugged one shoulder. "That's what moms are supposed to do. Take care of their children."

Another long silence, this one more than awkward. Tense. He was standing in the door to the hallway, leaning against the frame with his arms crossed over his chest. She would have to ease by him to leave. And she couldn't quite imagine doing that, couldn't imagine coming so close to him. Not dressed as he was.

Or as *she* was. She suddenly remembered what she had on—the white nightgown she'd brought with her from the trailer. She'd finally started wearing it because she hadn't wanted to keep sleeping in her clothes.

But she'd never expected to confront Wyatt in the middle of the night in it.

"I—I think I'll try to get some sleep," she said. Maybe he would move out of the way if she approached. He wouldn't want contact any more than she did.

When she got near to him, though, he didn't move. This close, he seemed even more in the way. "Excuse me?" she said. Her voice sounded breathy to her own ears. Weak, which was what she felt with him right there. Within reach. She might be furious with him, but that didn't mean she didn't want him.

"You're driving me crazy," he said, gazing down at her. "But I'm not going to touch you. Unless…"

"Unless?"

He straightened up. "Unless that's your choice."

Susannah took a breath, held it. This would probably be her last chance. How could she ignore it?

Breathing out, she reached for his hands and brought them to her shoulders. His palms settled on her bare skin, warm, a little rough. She placed hers on his chest, felt his muscles tense. "That's my choice."

Holding her gaze, he backed her out of the doorway and then shut the door to the hall. And locked it. "So be it," Wyatt said in a rough voice and pulled her against him.

This storm broke quick and fast. Desire rushed through her at the first touch of his lips against hers, the strong, sure stroke of his hands down her back. Slow and deep and hot, his kisses consumed her, owned her, devoured her as he explored the joining of their mouths.

Wrapping her arms around his waist, she held on and offered everything she had, everything she was. She could feel the heat of him, the strength of him—the thin fabrics they wore were hardly a barrier between their bodies. Pressed hard together, they might as well have been naked.

They weren't…but they could be. Susannah eased her hold and turned her head to the side. "Your room?" she murmured, breathing fast.

Wyatt's hands went still. His chest rose and fell sharply against her breasts, an erotic pleasure all its own. He kissed her temple, her cheekbone, the curve of her jaw. "No," he said quietly. "I'm sorry. I shouldn't have started this."

"No, you shouldn't have." After the first moment of shock, passion transformed into anger. "You have to decide what *you* want. Don't jerk me around."

"I don't mean to jerk you around, Susannah. But sometimes in life, what I want and what I can have are two different things." He let his hands fall to his sides. "I'm not as strong about that as I'd like to be."

"Work on it," she told him harshly out of her own immense pain. Then she walked away from him, crossed the hallway and returned to her room. Her only regret was that, with Amber asleep, she couldn't slam the door.

Chapter Eight

Susannah made breakfast the morning of the rodeo, serving up a continuous stream of pancakes, eggs and bacon for the entire crowd. The noise level in the dining room was almost as high as the degree of excitement with seven teenagers anticipating their opportunity to compete in a real, live show.

"I've never seen them eat so much," Ford said as he brought a serving bowl to her for more eggs. "You'd think they hadn't been fed all week. And we cooked steak last night!"

"It's a big day," Caroline told him, coming in for a refill on her pitcher of juice. "The high point of their summer." She gave a slight frown. "As long as no one gets hurt."

Garrett picked up a new bottle of syrup. "We'll have our good luck charm on site. With Rachel there, everybody will be fine." The doctor would be meeting them at the fairgrounds in Buffalo.

Susannah laughed at him. "You may be a little biased on that topic. But I like the general idea." She scraped a pan full of eggs onto the plate Ford held. "There you go."

Dylan came through the door with another platter. "Three requests for more pancakes. Don't hold your breath, but I think they're slowing down."

Blowing a wisp of hair out of her eyes, Susannah turned to the griddle. "Coming up." She'd noticed that, unlike the other adults, Wyatt wasn't ferrying food and empty plates, hadn't even taken a break in the kitchen to eat his own meal in relative peace. Knowing him, he was keeping an eye on Amber, making sure she got a good meal in the midst of all the teenaged commotion.

More to the point, he was avoiding her, as he had since that night in the kitchen last weekend. She'd been dodging him, as well, because it hurt too much to smile with him, all the while aware of how soon this period of their lives would be over. When the summer camp ended next weekend, she and the children would be settling into a new home, starting over in a new life. Which would be exciting, except for the fact that none of them wanted to leave.

"Susannah?"

She jumped at the sound of her name and whirled to see Garrett standing nearby. "I'm sorry. What did you need?"

"Your pancakes are burning."

"Oh, damn." At least Amber wasn't in the room. She flipped on the fan above the stove and switched off the burner. "Damn, damn. I'll have to clean up the griddle before I can make new ones."

"Don't worry about it." He put a hand on her arm. "They're all outside now, waiting to climb into the van and get to the show. Caroline is keeping an eye on Amber while Wyatt and Ford put the horses in the trailer. Let me help you load these dishes in the washer and we'll be ready to leave."

Susannah smiled in relief. "I'd hate to leave a dirty kitchen."

"I figured as much." As he rinsed plates and glasses,

he said, "Caroline tells me you've found a place to live in Casper and a job in a grocery store. That's real progress."

"I think so." She'd driven into town several times recently, getting her new life set up. With Travis still on the loose, Dylan or Garrett had come along, just in case. "The apartment is within walking distance of Nathan's school, and Amber's is on the bus route so I can take her there, which is the main thing I was worried about. We can make it all work."

"We'll sure miss you, though." He brought another stack of dishes to the counter. "The three of you have become part of the family over the summer."

"Thank you." Suddenly, there were tears in her eyes. "I have to admit, leaving will be…hard. The kids love it here. Not just because it's so beautiful and so comfortable." She tried to blink her eyes clear. "You and your brothers have been wonderful. I don't know what we would have done without each of you." Despite her efforts, her cheeks were getting wet.

Garrett stepped closer, as if he might give her a hug.

Susannah held up one hand to stop him, wiping tears with the other. She didn't want pity. "But we'll come visit, as friends do. When you're in Casper, you can stop by to see how well we're doing." She forced a smile. "And we will be. I plan to be store manager. It's just a matter of time."

"I have no doubt." He retreated to the dishwasher and shut the door. "You can do whatever you set your mind to." Looking around the kitchen, he saw the stack of pans waiting to be washed. "Do we have to finish those before we leave?"

"As long as you don't dock my pay, they can stay there."

They were still laughing as they stepped out onto the

front porch, where Wyatt was coming up the steps with Honey following him. He stopped as he saw them, and a spasm of pain passed across his face so quickly that Susannah almost believed she'd imagined the moment. Almost but not quite.

"We're ready to go," he said to the space somewhere between her head and Garrett's. "Amber's already buckled into my truck. I'm just going to put the dog inside and lock the doors."

With Dylan and Garrett taking the backseat with Amber, Susannah had no choice but to climb in the front beside Wyatt. The two brothers kept her daughter entertained—or maybe it was the other way around—so all she had to do was sit there for the twenty-minute ride to Buffalo, painfully aware of the man sitting only an arm's length away. Walking away from him would be one of the hardest things she'd ever done.

At the Johnson County fairgrounds, they connected with Rachel and then the whole group of them settled at the top of the bleachers just in time for the opening ceremony.

"The Buffalo Junior Rodeo Show is proud to present a special guest star for today's event," the announcer said over the loudspeaker. "Four-time national finals barrel-racing champion and rodeo queen Miss Marley Jennings will present the American flag!"

The introduction to the national anthem began as a palomino horse galloped into the arena, ridden by a woman wearing a bright red shirt and black chaps. Her long black hair flowed behind her in the wind as she circled the show ground. Then she turned into the center and held her horse motionless as the crowd sang the anthem. The constant Wyoming wind blew the flag in picturesque waves.

"She's so cool," Lizzie said. "I want to do that." The girl sat with Thomas on one side and Marcos on the other, with Nate occupying the bench behind her. Becky had managed to sit beside him, but he was leaning forward, paying attention to the blonde. Wearing her hair braided and just a light touch of makeup, Becky looked lovely. But Susannah wondered if her son was just too dazzled by Lizzie's wiles to recognize the redhead's kindness and more natural beauty.

Amber tugged on her shirtsleeve. "What do we get to see now, Mommy?"

Wyatt, on Amber's other side, answered. "Mutton bustin', Princess. Remember how that works?"

"Where you ride the sheep?"

"Right."

"I want to do that." She turned to Susannah and tugged on her shirtsleeve again. "Can I learn to do mutton bustin', Mommy? Please?"

"Not today, sweetie." A mother's eternal evasion.

Which didn't work with her daughter. "But Mr. Wyatt could help me and then I could come to the rodeo and ride a sheep. Please, Mommy?"

Ignoring the urge to glance at Wyatt, Susannah squared her shoulders, turned toward her daughter and took her hand. "I don't think we can do that, Amber. You know we won't be staying at the ranch much longer."

Amber frowned. "I don't want to move."

"But we have to, and there won't be sheep where we live. We'll find other fun places to go—playgrounds and swimming pools and ball games. You're probably old enough to play ball now."

"I don't care." Pulling her hand free, Amber got to her feet and moved to stand in front of Wyatt, her palms on his knees. "Please, Mr. Wyatt, can't we stay? I'll be good, I promise. I won't hurt your 'puter or use too much paper. An' I'll go to bed real early. Please can't we live with you?"

Susannah didn't wait to hear any excuse Wyatt might give. She stood and bent to pick up the little girl. "Let's go get a drink," she said and eased past a dozen knees, making her way to the aisle.

Halfway down the bleacher steps, Amber started to wail.

Not until they'd reached the parking lot and Wyatt's truck did Susannah realize he'd followed them. She shook her head at him.

"I'll unlock the doors for you." He pressed the remote key and then hesitated. "Are you sure there's nothing I can do?"

Angry words pushed against her lips. Hurt words, lonely and aching words struggled for release. Susannah clenched her jaws and shook her head again as Amber sobbed on her shoulder.

Wyatt inclined his head. His eyes were shadowed by the brim of his hat. "I'm sorry." He spun and walked back the way he'd come.

With tears in her eyes for the second time that morning, Susannah put Amber into the truck, climbed in beside her and set about trying to explain to her little girl why neither of them could have what they wanted.

MUTTON BUSTIN', GOAT TYING, breakaway roping—Becky got more and more nervous the longer she had to wait for her barrel-racing event to start.

At least she didn't have to wait as long as Marcos, Thomas and Lena did. Bull riding was the last event of the day. Nate's pole bending would happen after the steer wrestling.

She poked him in the back. "Are you nervous?" she asked him. "About riding?"

He shrugged one shoulder. "It's my first time, so there's not much chance that I'll win. I'd be pretty happy to get through without knocking a pole down, though. Blue and I have been together long enough for us to make a clean run." Because he was a nice guy, he said, "Are you nervous?"

She nodded. "I tipped a barrel over in my last two practice runs. I'm afraid I'm going to do the same thing here."

"It's all for fun," he said, watching a boy struggling to get the steer's three legs tied together. "If you don't enjoy it, there's not much point in doing it. Right?"

"Well, you also don't want to look stupid."

Nate leaned close and lowered his voice. "I've decided you were right—stupid is sitting down on an untamed bull and expecting not to get hurt."

He thought she was right! That was something, anyway. "Still, I'll be happy just to stay on my horse."

"Keep your heels down and your legs long," he said. "You're pretty steady in the saddle, so you'll do fine."

Did that mean he'd watched her ride? Was he giving her a compliment?

While she was trying to decide, Nate gazed past her and then got to his feet. "Looks like it's time for me to saddle up." Mr. Wyatt was standing at the end of the bench, waiting for him.

"Good luck," Becky told him. "I hope you have a great race."

He grinned at her. "Thanks." Leaning down, he tapped Lizzie on the shoulder. "I'm going to ride in a few minutes. See you later."

Without even glancing at him, she said, "Okay," and pushed some popcorn into her mouth.

He stood staring at her for a moment with a puzzled expression on his face. Mr. Wyatt called his name and he jumped and then sidestepped his way to the aisle. Lizzie was too busy giggling at something Thomas had said to notice they'd left.

When the pole-bending competition started, the first competitor was a girl. And the second, as well.

"So ol' Nate's riding against girls," Marcos said. "He's bound to win."

Lizzie punched him in the shoulder. "That's not true. Girls can beat boys."

Thomas shook his head. "Nah." For once, the two guys agreed about something.

The next two girls each knocked one of the poles down, which meant they were disqualified. Finally, it was Nate's turn. Coming out of the gate, he and Blue Lady streaked across the arena, pivoted sharply and started a zigzag pattern around the poles. Becky had seen him practice this over the last few weeks by weaving through the line of pine trees on the ranch.

With a press of his legs and a flip of the reins, Nate moved Blue from side to side, going one way and then, with another quick spin, coming back through again. The last pole wobbled as they went by a little too close, but Nate put out a hand to steady it. Then they were turning one more time and racing for the finish.

"He did it!" Becky jumped up, cheering. Lena and Justino joined her and even Thomas, Marcos and Lizzie made some noise. "Way to go, Nate!"

"That was first timer Nate Bradley," the announcer said, "with a score of twenty-two point five six seconds. Good job, Nate."

Becky turned to look at Ms. Caroline, standing behind her. "Is that a good score?"

"It's great for his first-ever ride. And I think that's the fastest time so far. But whether he wins or not depends on how the other competitors fare. We won't know until everyone has gone through. Meanwhile, though, we have to get the horses ready for your event. You and Lizzie will be up soon."

Between backing her horse off the trailer, cleaning him up and putting on the saddle, Becky missed the announcement for the winner of the pole-bending event.

She was tightening the cinch when Nate suddenly showed up. "Need some help?"

From bending over to tighten the knot, Becky straightened up so fast, her horse startled and shied away. "Did you win? Did you?"

"Whoa, there." Nate put a hand on the horse's shoulder and calmed him down. "As a matter of fact..." he said and grinned. "I did." He pulled a blue ribbon from his back pocket. "How about that?"

Without thinking, she threw her arms around him. "Congratulations! That's so cool!" For a second, she felt his hands on her back—a slight hug in return—but in the next moment his arms dropped to his sides. Feeling her face heat up, she stepped away. "I knew you could do it."

"So you won, huh?" Thomas came over. He'd been standing nearby, watching Lizzie get ready to race. "Not too hard, though, beating a bunch of girls."

"I heard that." Lena stalked over to glare at him. "You're going to wish you could beat a girl when I finish riding my bull." Justino, as usual, stood right beside her.

Thomas rolled his eyes. "They probably gave you the weakest one in the bunch. They're not going to let the little girl get hurt."

Considering that Lena was taller than him by a head, it was a dumb thing to say. "You talk so big," she told him. "But I'll make it to the whistle *and* get a higher score than you."

Hands on his hips, Thomas sneered at her. "What do you want to bet?"

"Kitchen chores. Whoever wins does the other one's work for the rest of camp."

"Done. And you'll be sorry when you're washing dishes all the time." He swaggered away to get a high five from Marcos and a grin from Lizzie.

"Maybe it's a good thing camp will be over soon," Becky commented to Nate. "Everybody needs their own space for a while."

To her surprise, he shook his head. "Not me. I wish camp could go on all year. Even if it means putting up with those two. I don't want to leave the Circle M. Especially not to live in Casper," he finished in a low voice. He glanced over at his mom, who stood by the front left door of the truck, watching Amber pretend to drive.

Before Becky could think of the right thing to say, Ms. Caroline came around the end of the trailer. "You two should start warming up," she said. "Let me check to be sure your cinch is tight."

Next thing Becky knew, she was in the saddle and her own nerves were taking over again. Walking, jogging, running—she put Desi through his paces, making sure his muscles were ready for the cloverleaf pattern they would follow. The warm-up area had barrels set up, and she rode around them in the right order but not up to speed, reminding herself that she did know how to do this. They'd been practicing all summer.

Lizzie went by her several times but never nodded or spoke. Becky wasn't sure what had happened to their friendship—something about the boys just seemed to make the other girl crazy. All Becky was sure of was that it was a sad way to end what had been a fun summer.

And then they were standing in a line outside the alley, waiting for their turns to ride. Becky's hands were sweaty on the reins, and her hat sat too tight on her head. With her luck it would fall off, her braid would come undone and her hair would get in her eyes and she wouldn't be able to see where they were going. Maybe Desi would remember the pattern without her?

Lizzie was in line ahead of her. She hadn't looked back even once. But Becky decided to make one last effort. "Good luck!" she called to her former best friend.

After a minute, Lizzie's shoulders lifted. She twisted around. "You, too." But she said it without a smile.

Sooner than Becky expected, Lizzie was next in line. She got the signal and kicked Major into a run, heading down the alley toward the arena. Ms. Caroline, standing with Mr. Ford at the fence, yelled, "Have fun!"

Feeling almost sick to her stomach, Becky moved Desi into position, just as Lizzie came jogging back down the alley. "Awesome!" she called out as she passed.

Becky faced her horse down the alley. Ms. Caroline yelled, "You can do it, Becky!"

The man on the fence beside her said, "Go!"

Pulling in a deep breath, Becky kicked her heels against her horse's sides.

And went.

AFTER HIS ENCOUNTER with Susannah, Wyatt decided to watch the show at ground level for a while. He couldn't face questions or comments from his brothers about Amber's plea to stay at the ranch.

He was having enough trouble facing his own self-reproach.

Watching Lizzie and Becky make their runs took his mind off his mistakes for a few minutes. Neither of them scored a winning time, but the fact that they raced at all said a lot about what had been accomplished on the ranch this summer. Considering that Lizzie had been scared to death of horses on the first day, having her trust her pony in a cloverleaf pattern at a run was something of a miracle. And Becky—

"If it isn't Wyatt Marshall."

He'd been expecting to run into her all day. Turning, he found her closer than he'd realized. "Hey, Marley. Nice to see you."

She laughed in that hearty way she had. "You always were the master of understatement. It's good to see you, too. What brings you to a youth rodeo? Do you have kids of your own competing?"

"I do." In a manner of speaking, anyway.

Marley tilted her head. "I'm glad to hear it." Her hair was still long and shiny black, her eyes a violet blue. He thought she was using more makeup than she once had. "I'm still competing, obviously. Still winning."

"So I hear. You've made a great career for yourself."

Her smile held a touch of regret. Or was that just his wishful thinking? "I imagine you're still running the Circle M."

"I am."

"Old man MacPherson got himself a treasure when he took you on. Nothing could pry you away from the ranch. Not even me."

"It was a tough contest, though."

"Don't lie," she said, laughing again. "And if I couldn't peel you away from the land, I damn sure couldn't separate you from those three brothers of yours. How are they doing?"

"Ford's a lawyer, Garrett's a minister and Dylan's an artist. Ford and Garrett are engaged. They're all fine."

"Hmm." Tapping a painted fingernail against her bright red lips, she stared at him for a moment. "Each one of them has a career outside the ranch. But not you? I seem to remember you wanting to go back to school..."

"I've been too busy."

She put her hand on his arm. "You can't fool me. You stayed because you didn't want to go anywhere else. You get what you want—what you need—from those square miles of Wyoming dirt. Only your brothers matter more."

That wasn't true anymore. Someone else mattered to him now. Someone for whom he'd considered breaking his oath...

"Marley Jennings!" Wyatt got pushed to the side as a gaggle of teenaged girls rushed down on them, pens and papers in hand. "Can I have your autograph?"

"Miss Jennings, can I take your picture?"

"Can you pose with me?" Becky and Lizzie were part of the mob.

Marley posed and signed and laughed, provided barrel-racing tips and wished them all good luck. "Part of the job description," she said as the crowd dispersed. "I wouldn't have it any other way." Gazing past him, she raised her eyebrows. "And who is this cowboy?"

Wyatt pivoted to find Nate just behind him, Susannah at his shoulder holding Amber. The three pairs of blue eyes were wide with surprise.

Nate held up his blue ribbon. "I won," he said, grinning. "Blue and I won."

"I saw that." Wyatt shook his hand. "It was a great ride."

Before he could introduce them all, Marley stepped in front of him. "It's good to meet you," she said, shaking hands with Nate and Susannah. "I'm an old friend of Wyatt's. We go back ten years and more." Facing him again, she put a hand on his shoulder. "I have to run— I'm presenting the ribbon for the bull-riding winner. It's been great visiting with you, darling." Going up on tiptoe, she gave him a kiss on the lips. "Take care of yourself. Hope I'll see you again sometime soon."

As she hurried away, Nate said, "You know Marley Jennings? That's too cool. She's famous."

"She was a lot less famous when I knew her." He met Susannah's gaze. "Were you planning to watch the bull riding from the bleachers?"

She nodded without saying anything, only shifting Amber a little higher onto her hip.

Wyatt held out his arms. "Want me to carry her up there?"

But Amber turned her head away from him, burying it in the curve between her mother's neck and shoulder.

Great. He'd lost his biggest fan.

He waited for Susannah to go ahead of him up the steps. At least he could catch them if they fell.

The bleachers were more crowded than they'd been all day—everyone wanted to watch the bull riding. Garrett had saved some space but just barely enough. Nate and the girls squeezed onto the front bench. Susannah sat next to Garrett with Amber in her lap, leaving Wyatt about half the room he needed. With apologies to the man on his other side, he sat down anyway.

Susannah kept her gaze on the arena but said, "So that's the woman who wouldn't stay?"

"Yes." Something more should be said. "As you can tell, we wanted different lives."

"You must have been very hurt."

"I thought I was at the time." The audience gave a collective groan as a competitor got thrown off his bull before the whistle. "I've since learned there's worse pain."

He waited, but she didn't answer.

Thomas was the first of the Circle M contestants to ride. He came out of the gate on a bull named Desperado. Wyatt could tell how much he'd learned over the summer in the determination with which he held onto the rope and kept his seat. Once the whistle blew, he tumbled off but scrambled out of the way as the clown distracted Desperado. The Circle M kids cheered as Thomas stood in the arena with his arms raised in triumph, his big grin visible even behind his face mask.

Marcos's bull was HiJinks, obviously named for the jumps and spins he put the boy through. Though his style wasn't great, Marcos held on through the whistle, which was more than most first-time riders could claim. He managed to land on his feet when he came off, but he had to run for the fence when HiJinks reeled to chase him down.

"Thank God for rodeo clowns," Garrett said as, once again, the clowns danced in to snag the bull's attention. "The hardest job in the show."

"Amen," Dylan replied. "They saved my butt more than once."

Whether by accident or design, Lena turned out to be riding the final bull of the afternoon. "This is Miss Lena Smith," the announcer informed them, "riding Bumble. Let's watch how a girl does it, folks."

"*Bumble* sounds like a baby cow," Susannah said. "Do you suppose they gave her an easy ride deliberately? She'll be furious."

Watching the bull banging around in the chute, Wyatt shook his head. "I doubt it."

The gate swung open and Bumble emerged spinning. He kicked and bucked and circled, throwing Lena around like a toy. The crowd gasped with every swing and tilt, expecting the worst, but the whistle sounded and she was still riding.

Wyatt stood up. "Her hand's stuck. She can't get free." In the next moment, Lena's left leg was thrown over the top of the bull and he started dragging her by one arm. The clowns closed in, soothing, slowing, distracting the animal. A sigh of relief went through the crowd in the bleachers when the rigging fell off and Lena dropped to the ground, lying facedown. Garrett and Rachel had already started toward the ground.

"That's one tough little lady," said the voice over the loudspeaker. "Miss Lena Smith, ladies and gentlemen. Give her a big hand."

But no one applauded until Lena moved. As Ford and the other men from the chute hovered around her, she got her arms under her and pushed up into a sitting position. In a few seconds, with Ford's help, she got to her feet. As those in the bleachers clapped, she managed to wave an arm and walk slowly out of the arena.

Nobody from the Circle M relaxed until they surrounded Lena, who had been checked out by the EMTs and by Dr. Rachel before being allowed to go to the truck. She sat sideways in the backseat, sipping juice and smiling. "I'm okay. Really."

Standing beside her, Justino looked worse than she did, his face still pale, his normally squared shoulders hunched. "Never," he said quietly. And then more forcefully, "Never again."

As the group quieted, Lena stared at him. "What are you saying?"

"I have endured this passion of yours," Justino said, his eyes blazing with anger. "All summer I have watched as you risked your health and your safety over and over for this...this stupid so-called sport." He made a cutting motion with one hand. "No more. You have ridden your last bull."

Silence reigned as she glared at him, her spine straight, her eyes narrowed. Wyatt crossed his arms, waiting for the inevitable outburst of temper. Ford sent him a knowing glance and a nod.

All at once, Lena subsided against the seat. "You're right," she said in a quiet voice. "I've done enough. I didn't win, but I rode to the whistle." She looked at Thomas. "And I got the best score out of the three of us."

"Yes, you did." Grinning, Justino put his arm around her shoulders. Then, heedless of the teenagers and adults standing there watching, he bent his head to hers for a kiss.

Everybody turned away, pretending they hadn't seen.

They all ate supper under the big tent where local scout troops were offering burgers and hotdogs, with brownies for dessert. Wyatt surveyed the long table and took the open spot he found between Amber and Becky, hoping to mend fences.

He settled in and gave the little girl a chance to finish the bite of hotdog she was chewing. "Did you have a good time at the rodeo?"

Swallowing, she nodded.

"Which event did you like best?"

She lifted her shoulders in a shrug. "Nate won the pole bending."

He missed the complete trust she'd once had in him. "The bull riding was pretty exciting, too."

Amber ate a potato chip. "I'm going to be a ballerina," she announced when she'd finished.

Wyatt glanced at Susannah, who was watching them out of the sides of her eyes. "When did you decide that?"

She crunched another chip. "My mommy said that I can't ride horses in my new house. But I can take lessons to be a ballerina. I'll dance with my arms like this." She raised her hands over her head in the classic pose. "And I'll twirl around."

"You will be beautiful," he told her. But the words left a bitter taste in his mouth. Lost dreams, missed opportunities…regrets for a future he'd declined burned in his gut.

"Guess I'm not too hungry," he said to Amber. "I'll meet you all at the truck when we're ready to go home."

Their return drive to the ranch was quick and quiet. The sun set behind the Bighorn Mountains on his right-hand side, and a lopsided moon came up on the left. Susannah sat in the backseat with her daughter, who fell asleep in a matter of minutes. Dylan sat in the front but didn't have much to say—though it had been weeks since his reporter had left, he still wasn't his usual carefree self. Wyatt didn't feel much like talking, anyway.

He stopped the truck in front of the house so Garrett could help Susannah unload Amber. The kids had gotten home first and were probably already asleep in their bunks. As he glanced at the front porch, though, he saw Honey standing there, wagging her tail.

When Garrett went to the front door, it opened with just a push.

Wyatt shook his head. "Something's wrong. I locked Honey inside before we left." He put the truck in gear.

"Let's get these horses settled and then we'll figure out what's going on."

When they went through the barn to the corral, however, they found the gate to the field wide open.

"What the hell?" Wyatt stared at Dylan. "I can't believe we left that gate unlocked this morning."

"It gets worse," Dylan said. "The corner gate is open, too. The horses could be anywhere in the county by now."

With the corner gate now shut, Wyatt went to the edge of the field and whistled for Caesar. No other horses were visible in the waning light. And Caesar, for the first time since he was a yearling, didn't answer.

"Take one of these horses," Wyatt told his brother, "and ride out to the far gate. I'm betting you'll find it's open, as well."

Not bothering with a saddle, Dylan swung onto Blue and loped across the pasture. In only a few minutes, he returned.

"You're right. The gate was open." He slid down from the mare's back. "And out of the whole herd, there's not a single horse in sight."

"Damn Travis Bradley," Wyatt growled. "Damn him!"

Chapter Nine

With Dylan and Ford, Wyatt spent most of the chilly night riding the rangeland of the Circle M underneath that flattened circle of a moon, searching for the missing animals. Bradley hadn't been content to simply open the gate—he must have spooked the horses and sent them running, away from their grassy field into the larger, more varied terrain of the cattle enclosures.

Or he could have sent them out the gate by the barn, down the drive and off the ranch altogether. Wyatt hated considering that possibility. Barbed wire posed a wicked threat to panicked equines, as did gullies, ravines and fallen trees. The image of Caesar, or any of the herd, lying in some ditch with a broken leg kept his gut churning all night. As the hours passed without success, though, he began to fear that Bradley really had been that malicious.

He returned to the barn about four in the morning, but he was already making plans to head out again in his truck as soon as it was daylight. He would call the sheriff, as well, though they had no proof that this was Bradley's doing. A careless kid could leave a gate open. But Wyatt was certain that wasn't the case this time. His horses wouldn't leave their grassy home without being sorely provoked.

With the chestnut unsaddled, brushed and turned into the corral with a pile of hay, Wyatt decided he had to get himself some coffee or fall asleep on his feet. Susannah would have left the brewer on.

What he didn't expect was to find her awake, seated at the kitchen table with Garrett. They both looked up as he came in, but neither asked how it was going. His face no doubt answered the question.

"You haven't eaten in hours," she said instead, standing. "Let me make you some food."

He started for the coffeepot, surprised that she'd noticed he hadn't bothered with dinner.

But she caught his arm and pulled him around. "I'll make your coffee. Just sit down."

Wyatt was tired enough that he did what she ordered him to. When she brought the cup, he gulped greedily and only afterward said, "Thanks."

"You ought to get some sleep," Garrett urged him. "At least a couple of hours."

Shaking his head, Wyatt drained off more of his mug. "What did he do in here?"

Susannah turned from the refrigerator holding eggs and bacon. "How did you know he'd been inside the house?"

"Honey was out. The door was unlocked." More coffee. "What's the damage?"

"He washed the pots and pans," Garrett said. "Left them drying on the counter."

"To taunt me." Susannah went to the counter and set down the food. "He always made fun of the way I liked to keep things neat." With her back to him, she braced her arms on the counter. "I am so ashamed to have brought this trouble into your lives."

"I'm going to check on the boys. Just because." Garrett threw Wyatt a pointed glance and then got to his feet and stepped quietly through the dining room door.

"Doing the right thing," Wyatt said slowly, "usually causes trouble, one way or another. That's simply how life works." He set down his mug and went to stand beside Susannah. "You've spent years doing the right thing—keeping the promises you made even when your husband didn't."

She took a deep breath and relaxed her arms, clasping her hands together in front of her on the counter. "I tried."

"This summer, he crossed the line of what you could accept. You chose to do the right thing for your kids, which meant leaving him. Given his nature, problems were inevitable."

"Yes. But—"

He put a hand on her shoulder. "My family did the right thing in offering you and Nate and Amber refuge. We didn't expect it to be easy or worry-free. But I'm certain that none of us would've chosen to act differently, if we had the chance. Knowing you, enjoying you and the children in our lives this summer, has been a privilege I…we wouldn't give up for anything."

A tear splashed on her knuckle. "You're very kind."

Wyatt barked a laugh. "Hell, Susannah, you know I'm not kind. I'm ornery and curt at the best of times, and right now is not one of those. But I tell the truth."

Turning toward him, she reached up and laid her slender palm along the side of his face. "You're a strong and decent man with a gentle heart. That's what matters." The shine in her eyes, the smile on those soft lips, said she loved him as plainly as if she'd spoken the words.

But how could he accept this gift she wanted to give at the expense of an independence she'd never had a chance to explore? Didn't loving her mean he owed her a life of her own choosing?

He squeezed her shoulder and then took a step back, away from her touch. "What matters is that we find Bradley and get him in jail where he belongs." So he wouldn't have to witness the change in her face, he walked to the table, picked up his mug and took a drink of cold coffee. "I'll talk to Wade Daughtrey tomorrow."

When he looked at her again, she was peeling apart strips of bacon. "I made biscuits earlier," she said. "I'll warm them up."

"Sounds good."

And to that useless comment she made no response at all.

As he finished his meal, Ford and Dylan came into the kitchen, neither of them having found a trace of the missing horses.

"Daylight will help," Ford said, rubbing his hands over his face. "Every clump of sagebrush resembles a horse in the dark."

"They're out there laughing at us." Dylan folded his arms on the table and put his head down. "Standing safe and sound in some secluded corner, listening to us yelling their names like fools." His Appaloosa, Leo, was one of the missing.

Susannah brought more food to the table. "You'll feel better if you eat something. What else do you need?"

"A good night's sleep," Dylan mumbled into his arms. Then he sat up and smiled at her. "You're a wonder, you know. Feeding cowboys at five in the morning after being up all night goes beyond the call of duty."

She ruffled his hair, as a mother would her son, before going to pick up the coffeepot and bring it to the table. "More?" she asked Wyatt without meeting his eyes.

"Thanks." Mug in hand, he got to his feet. "I'm going to take a shower and change, then head out in the truck at daylight, which shouldn't be too long now."

In fact, when he reached his bedroom, the blackness outside his window didn't seem quite so deep as it had been, and he could move around easily without switching on a lamp. The lack of artificial light soothed his tired eyes. Taking his shower in the dark brought relief to his aching muscles, too, and he felt almost optimistic as he dried off. They would find those damn horses, and they'd all be just fine.

Standing in front of his closet, however, he realized he couldn't choose his clothes in the dark, so he clicked on the light beside the bed. Squinting against the glare, he saw a piece of paper lying squarely in the center of the mattress. He had no doubt who'd put it there— Travis Bradley had left him a message.

If I can't have them, he had scrawled, *nobody can.*

As Susannah finished drying the last pan, the fiery-orange rim of the sun crept over the horizon, sending the first beams of daylight through the kitchen window. Time to get up…except she'd never been to bed.

She could, she decided, afford to rest for a few minutes before Amber awakened. Filling her coffee cup yet again, she carried it out to the front porch and sat in one of the rockers with Honey at her feet. Oh, how she would miss the beautiful, loving dog when they moved.

Then again, what wouldn't she miss about this special place? Dawn breaking over the plains to the east, painting the clouds with rose and gold? Or a brilliant sunset, the splashes of red and orange and purple a perfect backdrop to the peaks of the Bighorns? The rippling water of Crazy Woman Creek, where Amber loved to play, the endless stretch of grass pasture and the cattle grazing there? The cozy red barn, filled with the sweet scent of hay?

What about the Marshalls, themselves? Ford, with his incisive intelligence, his sharp blue eyes and unbeatable logic. Caroline, a soon-to-be Marshall whose care and concern had rescued her children from the menace of abuse. Garrett, intuitive and supportive but also wryly funny.

And Dylan, the charmer who, even with his heart broken, could always manage to boost a woman's spirits. She'd come to love them all. She would miss their daily presence with an ache that might never heal.

But, ah, Wyatt…her love for Wyatt had grown far beyond what she had imagined love could be. He had become as necessary in her life as her children. Like them, she really wasn't sure how she would manage without him.

She would, of course, though the prospect dismayed her. For her children, she would do anything she had to.

When Honey lifted her head and perked her ears, Susannah glanced toward the front door just as Wyatt stepped outside. He gave her a smile. "A little chilly out here, isn't it?" He still looked tired and stressed.

She raised her cup. "Warm coffee. Are you going out again?" The sun had popped up into the eastern sky, and the day was going to be a bright one.

"Toward the road," he said with a nod to the driveway leading off the ranch. "They could be running anywhere between here and the county highway. Or beyond. First, though, I thought I'd give this another try."

He stepped to the edge of the porch, put his fingers in his mouth and blew the whistle that summoned Caesar. And again.

In the morning silence, Susannah could have sworn she heard a faint horse's whinny. Judging by the tilt of Wyatt's head, he'd heard it, too. He signaled once more.

Another whinny, slightly louder. Like an approaching storm, the thunder of hooves sounded in the distance, a soft drumming that grew louder with the advance of a dust cloud along the driveway. Caesar's trumpet call, answering Wyatt's third whistle, was echoed by other equine voices.

And then Susannah could see them—a herd of horses galloping within the fog stirred up by their hooves. Caesar, pale as a ghost, held the lead. As she wondered how they would ever stop, Wyatt jogged down the porch steps and out into the middle of the drive going by the house, right in front of the approaching stampede. Legs spread wide, arms stretched out, he stood motionless before the onslaught.

With her heart pounding in her chest, Susannah jerked to her feet. What on earth could she do to help?

The screen door banged and Ford came out, hair wet, shirt hanging open over his jeans. "What the hell—?" His younger brothers stood behind him.

"Oh, my God," Garrett said, and it was a prayer.

But Dylan laughed. "Leave it to the boss."

Susannah couldn't close her eyes, though she wanted to. She had to see what happened.

In that moment, she could only believe that Wyatt would be killed. By his own galloping horse.

But then, with perfect control, Caesar slowed to a trot…to a prance. Finally, to a stop. Snorting, throwing his head from one side to the other, he stood an arm's length away from Wyatt, asking for approval. *Aren't you impressed? Didn't I do well?*

Behind him, the other horses milled around, blowing off steam. Among them, Susannah could see Leo, Dylan's horse; Ford's palomino, Nugget; and the black shadow that was Garrett's Chief. She didn't know the other horses as well, but she counted at least twenty.

"Is that all of them?" she asked Ford.

Nodding, he finished buttoning his shirt. "Apparently. Horses tend to stay together—they feel more secure in their herd. Now all we have to do is wrangle them back to the field."

"Mommy?"

Susannah turned to find her daughter standing at the screen door. "What in the world are you doing awake?" She went to pick up the little girl. "It's still early."

Amber snuggled into her shoulder. "I heard Caesar. I wanted to see him."

Shifting so the girl could have a full view of the horses, Susannah looked at Ford. "How will you move them?"

"There are four of us. We'll make it work, somehow." Then he glanced toward the bunkhouse and chuckled. "Well, how about that. We have help, after all."

Like Amber, the boys must have been awakened by the commotion and come outside to find out what was going on. Susannah checked out the cabin, where Caroline and the girls were up, too. Everyone was still in their pajamas, but they'd put on shoes.

And so what could have been chaos became fairly simple, with Wyatt leading Caesar toward the barn and all the kids plus Ford, Garrett and Dylan herding the other horses along behind them. Susannah followed, carrying a barefoot Amber. She watched with pride as Nate and the other teenagers drove the skittish animals up the hill with the confidence of experienced cowboys and cowgirls. Going around the corner of the barn and through the gate proved a little tricky—the horses wanted to crowd in all at once. But with the help of the Marshall brothers, the kids who had been nervous greenhorns at the beginning of the summer managed to funnel the herd through with real finesse. Wyatt opened the gate into their pasture, and with homecoming neighs, the horses reclaimed their familiar home. After a few minutes of cantering around, they all found a place to stop and settled in to graze.

"Whew." Arms propped on the top of the gate from the corral, now safely closed, Wyatt blew out a breath. "That was an adventure." He eyed the kids standing on either side of him. "My thanks to all of you for helping. It would have been a lot harder without you."

"How'd they get out?" Thomas asked.

"Yeah, especially in front of the barn like that," Marcos added.

"Somebody left the gates open," Wyatt said tersely.

"One of us?" Nathan demanded.

"No" was all Wyatt said.

But Travis's son understood. "*He* did this? *He* let the horses loose? When he knows…" His face white and drawn, he spun around and stalked across the corral.

Susannah started after him. "Nathan—"

But Wyatt stopped her with a hand on her shoulder. "Let me talk to him." He nodded toward Amber. "You take care of her. I'll handle this." He strode toward the barn.

And because she really had no idea what she would say, Susannah let him go.

Wyatt found Nate in the tack room, sitting on the couch with his hands gripped between his knees and his head bowed. "You okay?"

Nate shook his head. "How could he do that? He's a cowboy. He should care about horses. Not put them in danger."

How did you explain evil to a kid? "He had a different purpose in mind."

"To pester you?"

"Something like that." The note left on his bed was more than pestering. But the boy didn't need that detail.

"He's so messed up." He scrubbed his face with his hands. "I wish he was dead."

"No, you don't. I know for a fact he would haunt you the rest of your life."

Nate looked up at him. "I remember—your dad died when you were a teenager. Was he a good guy?"

"He had his problems. Like your dad, he drank too much."

"Did he hit you?"

"He yelled a lot when he was drunk. That last night…" Wyatt drew a breath. "The two of us had a fight. Then he stormed out and got in the truck, driving drunk. I remember wishing…wishing he wouldn't come back. And he didn't."

"That wasn't your fault. You didn't make him drink. Or drive."

"I should have had more patience."

"It probably wouldn't have mattered." Suddenly, Nate was the one giving advice. "My mom told me my dad and other addicts have demons inside them, driving what they do. Nobody else can change them—they have to want to make a difference for themselves."

"Your mom is a wise woman."

"You like her, don't you?"

Startled, Wyatt met his eyes. "Very much."

"I mean, in a romancey sort of man-woman way."

"Well…" He should've remembered kids always picked up more than you expected.

"'Cause if you did, we could stay, right? You and my mom could be together and Amber and I could live here with you. We would be part of the Marshall family."

"Nate." Wyatt sat down beside him. "I care about your mom. A lot. But she's coming out of a tough situation, and she deserves time to decide what she wants. Who she is, where she's going. Your dad hasn't given her much of a chance to do that."

"I don't know…" Nate frowned as he thought. "I mean, when he was drunk, things would be bad. But when he wasn't around, my mom was always in a good mood. We didn't have much money, but she kept coming up with fun things for us to do—stuff we could learn about, places we could go for the day or the afternoon to explore and play. She says we're the most important part of her life. Her job, she says, is to help us grow up and she wouldn't want to be doing anything else." He shrugged his thin shoulders. "Sounds to me like she's made her choice."

"Yes." Susannah was a strong and determined woman. He'd seen that from the beginning. "But—"

"It's okay. I get it. It's one thing to have kids around the place for the summer. It's something else to sign on for life." Standing up, Nate started for the door.

Wyatt got to his feet. "I'm sure it's hard to understand. But you and Amber are not the problem."

The boy stopped and turned around. "What else could it be? All you have to do is watch the way my mom looks at you to see how she feels. But because you're being all noble, she has to plan to do everything all by herself, like that will somehow make up for my dad's mistakes. She'd be better off—happier—here, with you. If you believe anything else, you're the one who doesn't understand."

Wyatt remained where he was as Nate left the tack room. Before he could define his thoughts, let alone his feelings, Dylan came through the door, a couple of halters in hand.

"I guess he told you," he said. When Wyatt glared at him, he shrugged. "I came to put these up and couldn't help hearing. Sorry."

"This—"

"Is none of my business," his brother agreed. "Although I've been trying to figure out why you'd want to torpedo your chance for happiness. I guess I understand a little better now."

"What exactly do you understand?"

"You believe you're to blame for Dad dying."

After a pause, Wyatt said, "I should have stopped him."

"You tried."

Another pause, while Wyatt took that in. "How do you know?"

"I heard you arguing. Ford and Garrett were snoring, but I was awake. And I got up."

"You saw?"

Dylan nodded. "He wanted to go out. You tried to stop him and he hit you, but you held on, till he took you down to the floor and punched you again. Hard. He left while you were still down."

Wyatt rubbed his fingers into his eyes. "You were just a little kid."

"Old enough to understand that what happened was not your fault. So you can stop punishing yourself. If I'd realized you were taking the blame, I would have said something years ago."

"Sometimes things don't get said."

"A bad habit of yours." Dylan clapped him on the shoulder. "So at this point maybe you could allow yourself the possibility of a future you want. Not just the future you got stuck with."

Before his brother left the room, Wyatt said, "Do Ford and Garrett know?"

"I told them the next day. There were bruises on your face to explain. But then he was dead and nobody wanted to talk about it…" He took a deep breath. "It was twenty years ago. Let's move on."

Great idea…

Wyatt followed his brother through the barn, thinking about Susannah's job, her apartment in Casper, a new school for Nate and dance lessons for Amber.

Unless it's already too late.

SINCE THEY'D BEEN to the rodeo on Saturday, Becky and the others had housekeeping to do on Sunday afternoon—the last time they would have to wash their sheets and clean their bathrooms. Lizzie complained through the whole ordeal, as she had every week.

"I hate cleaning." She flipped a dust rag across the coffee table in the living room. "If they'd said I would have to clean, I wouldn't have shown up for this dumb camp."

"It's not dumb," Becky protested. "You liked riding in the rodeo. You like trail rides on Major." She plugged in the vacuum cleaner. "And we're having a dance."

"The first decent thing we've done all summer."

Shaking her head, Becky turned on the vacuum. Lizzie swiped at the tables beside the couch and the armchair, and then she went to stand in front of the window. When she didn't move for several minutes, Becky switched off the noise. "What's going on?"

"The deputy is here again."

Becky joined her at the window. Mr. Wyatt, Mr. Ford and Ms. Susannah stood on the front porch talking to a man wearing a uniform. "I guess this is about the horses being loose."

"Can you believe Nate's dad did that? What a loser." Lizzie giggled. "That explains why Nate is such a loser."

"Nate is not a loser!" Becky clenched her hands into fists. "Don't say that."

"Compared to Thomas and Marcos, he's pretty lame."

"Why? Because he doesn't agree that beating somebody up is the way to win an argument?"

"Let's see." Tapping her temple, Lizzie pretended to think. "Marcos and Thomas—bull riding, where they could get killed. Nate—pole bending, where his competition is all girls. Sounds pretty wimpy to me."

"That's harsh," Lena said from the kitchen area where she was straightening up the supplies she used to take medicine for diabetes. "He's just a nice guy. Quiet."

"Like Justino says so much." Lizzie was still staring out the window, though nothing had changed. "He's worse than Nate."

Lena stared at her with narrowed eyes. "Are you saying Justino is a wimp?"

Lizzie's only answer was to shrug one shoulder.

"What is your problem?" Becky whirled to stare at her. "Do you want to make us all mad? Why? You didn't used to be so mean. What in hell are you trying to do?"

Lizzie stood there for a minute with that superior expression, the one she'd been wearing for the last few weeks while she flirted with Thomas and Marcos and Nate.

Then, suddenly, she sat down on the couch and folded up over herself, hiding her face.

"I can't do it," she moaned. "I can't."

Becky sat down beside her. "Can't do what?"

After a pause, she said, "I can't go home." She pulled in a shaking breath. "They don't want me, never have. I'm just a mistake they got stuck with."

Lena gave a sarcastic laugh. "Oh, *I'm* wanted—for cleaning house and babysitting. I'd rather be ignored." She sat down in an armchair. "It will be hard, though. Leaving. Not just because it's been fun. People here care."

Becky recalled the chaos of her own home, the never-ending anger. "At least we've seen what it can be like now. I mean, if we'd never come here, then we wouldn't know it's possible for people to care. Well, except on TV shows. It's as if we've kinda been living in our own special story."

Lizzie lifted her head. "But now we've been canceled. We have to go back to real life. And be miserable."

"But this is real life, too." Becky paused for a moment, thinking about what she was trying to say. "The Marshalls and Ms. Caroline, Ms. Susannah…they're *always* this way. They'll always care about people. About us. So we might not be here every day, but we can hold onto what we have here. It's not going to change just because we happen to be someplace else."

"Like me and Justino," Lena said. "We're in love even if we're miles apart."

"Exactly. Friends stay friends, even when they don't see each other. Right?"

Lizzie sighed. "I guess so. It would be neat if we could come visit the ranch sometimes. Just to remember the good stuff."

"Somebody would have to drive us," Lena pointed out. "Unless you want to walk five miles from town. It'll be two years before Justino gets his license."

"Three for me," Becky said mournfully.

Lizzie buried her head in her arms. "It sucks to be thirteen."

With the cleaning done on Sunday, Monday was a much better day, thanks to a trail ride to a part of the ranch they'd never visited before, way up in the foothills of the mountains. Becky was pretty used to seeing eagles and hawks flying overhead on these trips, and they'd sometimes encountered deer, but this was the first time they'd come across an elk grazing on the side of a hill. Though they all tried to be quiet, when the big animal caught sight of them, it lumbered off into the trees.

They'd brought sandwiches along for lunch, thanks to Ms. Susannah, and spent the afternoon fishing in a lake bigger than any of those they'd visited so far. The fish were smarter, too, and refused to be caught, which made Thomas and Marcos sulk on the ride home.

Instead of going back the way they'd come, Mr. Ford and Mr. Dylan led them in a different direction, across some of the ranch's wilder terrain not fit for grazing cattle. They traveled through rock-strewn gulches and underneath giant trees and across ground more gravel than grass. Lizzie seemed a little tense, but Becky loved every minute of the challenging ride.

Late in the afternoon, they came out on a stony ridge on the far side of the ranch house and the barn, which could be seen in the near distance. Heading toward a clump of trees and the promise of a break in the shade, Mr. Ford suddenly put up his hand, the signal for everybody to stop.

"Is it a snake?" Marcos asked from behind Becky. "It's about time we came across a nice, fat rattler."

As she drew closer to the leaders, though, she realized it wasn't a snake. "Trash," she said over her shoulder. "Beer bottles and wrappers and junk." She urged her horse closer to Mr. Dylan's. "Should we pick it up?" she asked. "There's room in the trash bag from lunch." Marcos groaned. "It won't take long," she told him.

To her surprise, Mr. Ford shook his head. "We'll leave it just as it is. I don't want him to know we've been here." His voice had gone serious, and she took another look at the scene. It almost seemed as if someone had been camping there. Which would be trespassing, but the Marshalls didn't seem to mind too much.

Then she gazed across at the ranch again. Sure, it was far away, but, with binoculars or a telescope, you could probably make out pretty well what was going on. You could probably watch people coming and going...

Nate's dad had been spying on the ranch, she suddenly understood. He'd waited until they all left, and then he'd released the horses.

"Don't worry," Mr. Dylan said to her in a low voice. "Now we can find him, and we'll take care of it."

But Becky was more worried about Nate. He'd ridden on ahead, underneath the trees on the other side of the trash, and was sitting there on his own. Did he want company?

Did she care?

Carefully avoiding the trash, she circled around to join him in the shade. Before she could say anything, he lifted a hand. "It's okay. I'm okay." He did look calm, not destroyed as he had the day his dad had let the horses out.

She relaxed in the saddle. "Mr. Dylan says they'll take care of it now that they know where he's...hiding."

"I hope so," Nate said. "I hope they catch him soon." He blew out a breath. "Before he does something we'll all be sorry for."

Chapter Ten

Tuesday dawned hot and dry, making it the perfect day for painting T-shirts for the dance.

Susannah gathered with the teenagers, Caroline and Amber in the bunkhouse, where Thomas gave a presentation about the signs Native Americans used to decorate their horses. He'd prepared drawings of the different symbols and explained each of their meanings. The kids were going to use those characters on the oversized shirts they would be wearing to represent their horses at the dance.

"It's kind of a crazy idea," Caroline said to Susannah as they watched the campers planning out their designs. "But they're having fun with it. Who would have guessed?"

"I'm still amazed at how we could order all those different colors of shirts on the internet and have them delivered right to the ranch." Susannah shook her head. "The glow-in-the-dark fabric paints, too. There doesn't seem to be anything you can't get online. I guess I'll have to figure out how to buy a computer for Nathan and Amber to use at home. It seems to be pretty much a requirement these days, even for the youngest ones. I don't want them to fall behind, like their mother has."

"So you've registered them at their new schools in Casper?"

"I went down yesterday, with Wyatt as my body-guard." And a very uncomfortable trip it had been. She'd have gone by herself, but he insisted on coming along, only to spend nearly the whole drive in silence. What had once been a sustaining friendship was now a source of painful longing. But she was trying to move on. "I'm hoping they'll settle in without too much trouble."

"I hope so, too." Caroline lowered her voice. "Now that we know where Travis has been hiding—at least one of the places—we have a chance of catching him and making your life more secure." Ford had gone into Buffalo to talk to the sheriff earlier this morning. The other brothers were intent on their own tasks—Garrett had his regular office hours at the church, and Wyatt and Dylan were in the barn with a sick horse.

Susannah glanced at Nathan, who sat at the far end of the table, focused on his painting. She turned her back to him, to be sure he couldn't hear. "I hate to picture Travis in jail. But I hate to think of him sitting out there, watching us. I didn't realize he would react with such hostility when I asked for a divorce." A deep sigh escaped her. "And I hate that I've dragged others into my problems."

"That's what friends are for. The Marshall brothers are good friends to have."

"Not to mention the future Mrs. Marshalls." Susannah pretended to frown. "Or is that Mrs.-es Marshall?"

"Grammar was never my best subject. I get your point." She enveloped Susannah in a quick hug. "The feeling is mutual." Then she laughed. "I'm afraid Amber has forgotten which shirt she's painting—the one on the table or the one she's wearing."

"Uh oh." Susannah checked out the mess. "Um…yes. White handprints on a pink shirt. Very artistic. Also white cheeks, forehead and hair. I predict a bath in the near future." The black shirt on the table in front of Amber had also gotten its share of sponged-on white. "That looks sort of dappled, right? She wanted her horse to be like Caesar."

"Close enough." They walked around the table, surveying the different projects. "I think all these shirts are fantastic."

When they returned to Amber, the girl stood up from her chair. "I'm hungry, Mommy. What can I have to eat?"

Along the length of the table, seven heads lifted. "Me, too," Marcos said, echoed by several other voices. "Cookies?" Lizzie said hopefully, and Lena rolled her eyes.

"I'll see what I can come up with," Susannah promised. She went to the door, and Amber came after her.

"Can I go with you? I want to help."

"Okay." She could wash Amber's hands and face while they were at the house. "We'll be back in a few minutes."

Outside, as she headed down the hill with Amber a couple of steps in front of her, Susannah glanced toward the house, and her heart stopped. Then started pounding.

Travis's blue truck sat in the drive.

"Amber. Come here." She kept her voice down as she scanned the yard. Where could he be?

Singing a song of her own composing, her little girl continued to skip down the hill. Susannah raised her voice. "Amber, we have to go inside. Come to me. Now."

Finally hearing the urgency in her mother's voice, Amber obeyed. But she asked, "Why?"

With a death grip on her sticky little hand, Susannah hurried her back toward the bunkhouse. "Because."

"Because why?"

Without answering, Susannah glanced up toward the barn…and there he was. Standing at the door, staring inside.

Pointing a gun.

WATCHING CAESAR MUNCH a mouthful of hay, Wyatt leaned against the frame of the stall door. "He's eating fine now."

Dylan stood beside him, shaking his head. "But he walked away from his grain *and* hay at breakfast. After that tricky colic he went through this spring, I figured we ought to be careful."

"I'm not arguing. What did he do instead of eating?"

"Stared off into the distance, as if there was something out there to be worried about. I couldn't see what he could, of course."

"Well, he seems fine right now. We'll keep him inside for a while and watch him in case anything changes." He clapped his brother on the shoulder. "Thanks for—"

"Hey!" The shout came from the front of the barn. "That you, Marshall?"

Wyatt looked at Dylan and put up a finger for silence. Then he walked into the aisle and strolled toward the doorway. "What are you doing here, Bradley? I told you to stay off my property."

Travis Bradley stood just outside the door. He wore the same clothes he'd had on the last time Wyatt had seen him, but they were dirty and wrinkled now, with his shirttail out and his hair a mess. His arms hung by his sides.

"Your property. Big deal." His laugh held an edge of panic. "I've been on your land for weeks, and you didn't even know it. I've been watching everything you and that wife of mine have done." His words were slurred, as if he'd been drinking.

"What do you want?"

"I want my family. Where are they?"

Wyatt kept the very thought of Susannah, Nate and Amber being close by out of his mind. "Why?"

Bradley rolled his eyes. "We belong together. They're my kids. And she's mine, you hear? She's my wife."

Stalling, Wyatt propped a hip on a nearby hay bale. "You've been rough on them."

"I'll change, I told Susie I would. I just need a steady job. A man's not worth a damn without work to do."

"You're right. But you have to be dependable. A boss has to be able to count on you."

He hung his head. "I gotta stop drinking. And I will, when I have my family back." His head came up and then his right arm, holding a pistol. "Tell me where they are."

Wyatt didn't move. "Don't be stupid."

"I'm serious. I'm taking them with me. Today."

"And where are you planning to go? The sheriff is after you, Travis. You're not going anywhere they won't find you. Especially with two kids in tow."

"We're going out of state. They won't bother finding us in Arizona. They got better things to do."

"Maybe not." Wyatt got to his feet. "But I will."

Bradley narrowed his eyes. "You mean—"

"Travis?"

Wyatt winced to hear Susannah's voice.

Bradley turned his head, but that pistol arm didn't waver. "Hey, Susie. I'm here for you and the kids."

She came within Wyatt's range of sight. Alone, thank God.

"What are you doing?" Her fingers lighted on his left arm. "You're not thinking straight."

"I'm fine." He lifted his free hand to her face. "Let's find Amber and Nate and get the hell out of here. I've got plans for us."

"What kind of plans?"

Smart. Keep him talking. Wyatt smothered a grin.

"Arizona, baby. There's construction jobs down there, bosses begging for workers. No more cold weather, no more snow. Summer year-round. It'll be great."

"That does sound great, Travis. We can go…but you have to leave Wyatt alone."

Bradley glanced over. "You go get the kids. I'll deal with him."

"They're in the house, Travis. Come with me and we'll put them in your truck." She tugged at his arm. "Let's go. Before something happens."

"Okay, okay." He gestured at Wyatt with the pistol. "You're coming, too. Get out here."

Not finding an alternative, Wyatt did as he was told, being careful not to look at Susannah.

The pistol poked into his side as he walked beside Travis Bradley, down the hill to the empty house. They were almost out of time.

At the front steps, Wyatt paused, noting the dust cloud approaching on the drive from the front gate.

Travis shoved the pistol more firmly into his ribs. "Go on." Then he followed Wyatt's line of sight. "What's that?"

"The sheriff, I imagine," Wyatt said.

Swearing, Bradley pulled Susannah toward the blue truck. "Get in. Come on."

"You'll never make it," Wyatt told him. "The sheriff's got at least three cars with him. Give it up, Travis."

"No way." Now he had Susannah in front of him, his

arm around her waist, the gun shaking at her temple. "They'll let us through. They'll have to."

Wyatt's guts curdled inside him, but he kept his voice calm. "They won't, and you'll end up dead. Or in jail for the rest of your life. Is that what you want, Travis? Are you ready to throw everything away? You've got a choice here. Make the right one."

Bradley squeezed his eyes shut and then opened them as three sheriff's vehicles slid to a stop behind the blue truck, dust billowing around them. Coming up behind, Ford pulled his truck off to the side and the sheriff jumped out. Doors opened on the other cars and eight deputies got out, weapons drawn.

"Put the gun down," Wade Daughtrey ordered. "Let her go, Travis, and lower your weapon."

All at once, Bradley wilted. Shoulders slumped, head hanging, he lowered the pistol. His arm fell away from Susannah's waist. The deputies started forward.

In the next second, Wyatt was there to draw her free and wrap her in his arms. "You're okay," he murmured against her hair. "You're okay."

She pushed back far enough to gaze up at him. "*You're* okay," she said. "I was terrified when he pointed that gun at you."

He managed a half smile. "I know the feeling."

Dylan joined them. "Glad things shook out alright. I was betting on you to jump him, Boss."

"Thought about it," Wyatt said. "Didn't want to hurt my back." He watched as Travis was led away in handcuffs. Susannah kept her face averted. "Maybe we should go inside," he said quietly. "Let you sit down."

As they crossed the porch, though, she gasped. "Amber is probably scared to death. I didn't explain, just pushed her inside…the kids wanted snacks…"

"The kids won't starve." Wyatt opened the screen door. "And Dylan will walk Amber down here."

"Consider it done." Dylan took off up the hill.

Susannah's pale face finally regained its color when she sat on the sofa with her daughter in her lap. "I'm fine," she assured Amber. "Everything is going to be just fine."

Standing across the room, Wyatt recognized the shift that had happened inside him during the last hour, a newly awakened appreciation of life's possibilities. The ranch, the land and its animals, would always be a constant in his world. His love for his brothers and the families they created would never wane.

But living meant changing, and changing required choices. He could spend his life as he had for years now—trudging through the days, meeting his responsibilities with dedication but little joy.

Or he could accept the happiness that had blossomed when Susannah Bradley walked into his life. Did he deserve it? Maybe not. Concluding that he was willing to deal with the uncertainty, Wyatt could only be grateful for the opportunity and make the most of it.

If she agreed, of course. He still believed she should be able to choose the kind of future she wanted. Whatever she decided, he would abide by.

Until he could figure out how to change her mind.

BECKY WOKE UP on Friday and went to look out the front window. "No! It can't rain today!"

Lizzie came to stand beside her. "We can't have the dance in the rain. And we can't postpone it—we're going home tomorrow."

Lena was in the kitchen, giving herself her morning insulin shot. "Maybe it will stop. Just because it's raining now doesn't mean it'll go on all day. The storm could blow over."

But the rain continued, sometimes in sprinkles, sometimes pouring down. Becky spent the morning with Ms. Susannah, Amber and Nate in the kitchen at the ranch house, making oatmeal cookies and chopping vegetables while listening to the patter of water on the roof. Everybody was depressed at lunch, complaining about the weather and the start of school in just a few days. Underneath it all was the awareness that this was the last day of camp, something nobody seemed happy about. The shirts they'd painted hung on the walls of the living room, reminders of the fun they expected to have. Would they even get to wear them?

They'd planned to set up for the dance in the afternoon. But instead, they all went to the barn and sat around on the hay bales, watching water fall from the sky.

"This sucks," Thomas said. "We might as well go home today."

"We can at least have a fire in the ranch house tonight," Lizzie told him. "And sing songs and make s'mores at the fireplace. That'll be better than leaving."

"We did a bonfire this week already at the creek," Marcos reminded her, "and made s'mores. Tonight was gonna be different."

Lena nodded. "Tonight was going to be special."

"Why couldn't we have the dance anyway?" Nate asked in his quiet voice.

They all stared at him and Thomas said, "You want to do a rain dance, go ahead."

"Where are we?" Nate glanced around and held up his arms. "What's wrong with having it here?"

Marcus snorted. "We're gonna dance on top of the

hay bales?" A pile of at least a hundred bales occupied the center of the open area.

"We were going to move them outside anyway," Nate pointed out. "We could stack them against the walls and give ourselves room. It's a big space."

"We'll have to ask the grown-ups," Becky said. "But I bet they'll say yes. And they could even put up the lights we were going to use inside. We could have the dance in spite of the rain." She looked at Nate and grinned. "You're a hero."

He rolled his eyes. "It was pretty obvious, if you thought about it for a minute. So where's a grown-up we can talk to?"

They trooped through the rain to the ranch house, where they found Mr. Wyatt, Mr. Garrett and Mr. Dylan in the dining room, having some sort of meeting that involved papers spread all over the table. Mr. Ford and Ms. Caroline had gone into town for work this morning.

"Sorry to bother you." Nate had somehow become the speaker for the group. "We were just wondering…" He explained his idea. "We'll move all the bales our-selves. If that's okay."

The three brothers shared a quick glance. "Sounds like the right solution," Mr. Wyatt said. "One of us should have come up with it."

Mr. Dylan nodded. "As soon as they let me loose here, I'll be out to help." He made one of his comical frowns. "Ranch paperwork is not my specialty."

"Mine neither." Mr. Garrett straightened a stack of paper in front of him. "I'll be there when we're finished. Before sundown, I hope." He grinned at Mr. Wyatt, who only shook his head.

The rain didn't let up, but somehow the day became brighter as they headed back to the barn and set to work.

At the beginning of the summer, moving hay had seemed like work, but today they all laughed as they dismantled the big stack in the center of the floor and arranged the bales along the walls. Marcos and Thomas could lift the heavy blocks higher than anyone else, so they worked at the top till the rows were about five bales high. Lizzie was a little bit of a wimp about the process, but she and Lena together managed to move their share. By the time Mr. Dylan, Mr. Garrett and Mr. Wyatt appeared, the center of the barn was empty. And not only empty, but swept free of loose hay, thanks to Nate and Becky.

Hands on her hips, Lizzie smiled as she looked around. "Now there's room to dance!"

By the end of the afternoon, strings of lights stretched around their new "dance hall," as they started calling it, and long tables were set up for the food. Couches made of hay bales lined the walls, separated by tables also made of bales. Mr. Dylan brought over his music system so Lizzie could plug in her phone, filling the barn with sound. Ms. Susannah had gone to Casper and come back with a truck full of helium-filled balloons in the same colors as the paint they'd used on their shirts— bright red, white, green and blue. The balloons floated to the ceiling, their colored ribbon tails hanging down and blowing in the breeze that came through the barn door. Green tablecloths went over the tables, with green plates and cups to match.

"Grass-green for your make-believe horses," Ms. Susannah said. She'd also brought them all a snack of cheese and crackers and orange slices. "You have to last until seven for dinner. When the dance starts."

With everything done, they all just stood for a minute, staring.

"Look what we did," Becky said.

"Pretty amazing," Nate agreed. "I never dreamed it would turn out so well."

Marcos was in a good mood, for once. "The best dance I've ever been to."

Thomas gave him a shove. "You've never been to a dance."

"Hey." Marcos shoved the other boy back. "That's what I said."

The rest of them groaned, and left the barn to get themselves ready.

Becky thought they might look weird when they all returned to the barn—the extra-big shirts decorated with the painted symbols were not your usual party outfits. They'd made shirts for the grown-ups, as well, so all of them were dressed as their favorite horse—Mr. Garrett in black, Mr. Dylan in black spots on white for his Appaloosa, Leo, Mr. Wyatt and Amber in dappled white on black, and Mr. Ford and Ms. Caroline in gold for their palominos. Ms. Susannah wore pure white, for Caesar when he turned gray, she said. "When he's an old man."

So, okay, maybe it wasn't the most fashionable dance ever. But their outfits connected them all in a way that nice clothes wouldn't. Like the horses they'd been riding all summer, they'd become a herd, depending on each other for protection, for survival. They hadn't always gotten along, but they'd stuck together. That was a pretty big deal.

Becky's shirt had brown spots, like Desi the Appaloosa. Or like her freckles. Even a few weeks ago, she wouldn't have been comfortable drawing attention to herself that way. She would have remembered her mother's taunts and tried to avoid the whole idea.

But Desi's spots were beautiful. And, she'd learned, her freckles were not something to be ashamed of. Managed, maybe, with a little makeup, but she was who she was—a barrel racer, a party planner, and, most important, a loyal friend. When she went home, she would use the memories of this summer to guard her heart and soul.

For right now, though, the music was playing loud and Lena and Justino were already dancing. Thomas and Marcos had filled their plates and were sitting on one of the hay-bale sofas, eating.

"Boys," Lizzie said with disgust. "As if we came here to stuff our faces."

"Well, it *is* dinnertime." Becky's stomach growled. "I'm kind of hungry, myself." Besides, who would dance with her? Nate had helped Amber get some food and was sitting with her as she ate. "Might as well join the crowd."

As she edged her way around the dance floor, Mr. Dylan stopped her. "Will you dance with me?"

She stared at him. "Why?"

"I like to dance. And you're right here." He tilted his head. "Are you too cool to dance with a grown-up?"

"Um... I guess not." A little embarrassed, she moved out into the open, away from Lena and Justino. When she turned to face Mr. Dylan, he was already dancing.

He was good, too, but not in an old person's style at all. He moved like the guys on TV. Then Mr. Garrett and Dr. Rachel came onto the floor, followed by Mr. Ford and Ms. Caroline. With so many people around her having a good time, Becky stopped being self-conscious and joined in the fun. Maybe Nate would get the hint?

She and Mr. Dylan danced through three or four songs before they agreed they were ready for something to eat. Then, just as she finished her food, Marcos walked up.

"I'll dance with you, if you want to," he said, avoiding meeting her eyes.

Becky had to laugh. "Is that an invitation?"

Now he glared directly at her. "What else? Do you want to?"

"Sure, Marcos. I'll dance with you." As she went to throw her plate away, she saw Thomas still sitting with Lizzie. He was sulking, saying nothing, while she leaned toward him, talking.

"What are they arguing about?" she asked Marcos as they faced each other out on the floor.

"He won't dance." Marcos shrugged. "She's pretty mad about it."

Poor Lizzie. "Can't you convince him?"

Marcos gave her a disbelieving stare. "Why would he listen to me, of all people?"

"You could give it a try," she told him. Marcos just rolled his eyes.

After a couple more songs, Ms. Caroline turned down the volume on the music. Standing beside the sound system, she held up her hand. "Now seems like a good time for the apple-bobbing contest. We've got a big bucket over there filled with water and apples. The contestant who can pick up the most apples—without their hands—in two minutes will be the winner. We've got a special T-shirt as a prize—a Buffalo Youth Rodeo shirt signed by all of us who've been here at camp with you this summer."

Lizzie stood up and came into the center of the floor. "There's also a secret prize," she announced. "The kids all know what it is. Go for it, guys."

With a surprised expression on her face, Caroline nodded. "Let's get started. Who goes first?"

Marcos stepped up. "I'll do it." He went to the bucket

and knelt down, his hands behind his back. The rest of the kids gathered around.

Mr. Ford held up a stopwatch. "Ready, set, go."

Watching Marcos try to bite an apple in the water was as funny as they'd thought it would be. His hair got soaked right away, along with his shoulders and the neck of his shirt. Every time he tried to grab an apple, it popped away from him. He growled, and went after another one, without success.

"Done!" Mr. Ford said. "Sorry about that, Marcos. Who's next?"

Justino raised his hand. "I'll go." He winked at Lena. "Get ready."

But his luck was no better than Marcos's, and he ended the two minutes without grabbing an apple. When he went to stand by Lena, she whispered something in his ear and he grinned.

"Any of you girls going to try this?" Mr. Ford asked. "It's not just for the boys."

"Too messy," Lizzie said, and Becky nodded. She'd worked too hard on her braid to ruin it.

Lena pulled her hair back behind her shoulder. "I'm not getting wet."

"Then Thomas, I guess it's your turn. Step right up."

He hesitated, and Lizzie gave him a little shove, pushing him toward the bucket. With a roll of his eyes he stepped forward and then got down on his knees. "I hope it's worth it," he muttered.

"Go!"

Thomas dove into the bucket and came up almost right away with an apple in his teeth. As the crowd around him clapped, he twisted around and dropped it on the floor, and then he went back in but couldn't snag another one.

"One's better than none," he bragged, getting to his feet. "I'm feeling like that's a win."

"We've got one more contestant to go," Mr. Ford said. "Come on, Nate."

The cloudy day made the barn darker than usual, and, even with the lights strung around the walls, the glow-in-the-dark paint they'd used on their shirts had really started to show up. Nate came toward the bucket, his grayish-blue shirt painted with broken arrows, the symbol of peace; feathers, meaning power; and the box-within-a-box sign, which signaled good luck in hunting. Kneeling in front of the bucket, he took a deep breath.

Mr. Ford said, "Go!"

Instead of splashing down, Nate went in gently, staying above the surface of the water, and he got an apple almost right away. Now he and Thomas were tied.

"A minute left," Mr. Ford announced.

Nate stayed with his method but wasn't getting lucky. He straightened up, pulled in another breath and went back for one more try.

Mr. Ford started counting down the seconds. "Eight, seven, six…"

"You can do it, Nate," Amber yelled.

And with two seconds left, he did, raising his head with the apple in his mouth.

Thomas scowled, but everybody else cheered. Nate dropped the apple and got to his feet, grinning.

"Here's your shirt," Ms. Caroline held up a red T-shirt with signatures of all the grown-ups on it in black. "Congratulations. But what's this about a secret prize?"

"That's right." Lizzie went to stand beside Nate, smoothing down her hair. "We decided the winner gets to kiss the girl of his choice." She smiled at the boy next to her. "Who will that be, I wonder?"

"I don't know about this—" Mr. Wyatt said.

Nate could kiss Lizzie—she obviously expected him to. But Becky couldn't imagine him embarrassing himself in front of everyone like that. She figured he would take the easy way out and give his sister a kiss, since her shout had urged him on. That was the kind of thing he would do.

So she was looking at Amber and didn't realize he had moved…until he stood right in front of her.

"Hey," he said.

She frowned at him. "What are you doing?"

He put his hands on her shoulders. "This."

And he leaned forward and kissed her on the lips.

Chapter Eleven

"I can't believe it." Susannah had just watched her son kiss a girl. In front of the entire camp. "What's gotten into him?"

"Love, maybe." Wyatt was standing right behind her. "He woke up and realized what a prize Becky is." After a moment, he said, "Takes some guys a long time to figure things out."

"He's too young to be in love." She watched Nate and Becky dance to a slow tune. Becky's face absolutely glowed with happiness. "I'm not ready for him to grow up." After a talk with Marcos, Thomas had allowed Lizzie to drag him onto the floor, where they were draped over each other like a couple of blankets.

"I don't think you get a choice in the matter. But you've still got some time. He won't be getting married just yet." Wyatt's voice was low and easy, not tense in the way it had been for the last few weeks.

But, then, he'd been a different man altogether since Travis's arrest on Tuesday, more the assured and settled rancher she'd first come to know. He was out of the house a good deal during the days, slowly returning to his ranch duties. But when he was at home, he'd been more relaxed, more jovial than she could ever remember. He'd coaxed Amber into playing Candyland with him as well as sharing her coloring book. They'd been reading together before bedtime, and it was safe to say they were once again friends.

Of course, that was actually a pretty big problem, since she and the kids would be leaving tomorrow.

Susannah's throat tightened as she imagined driving away from the ranch and not coming back. But once camp ended, she had no excuse for staying. Their apartment in Casper was ready for them. She didn't have to be afraid of Travis anymore—this time she'd pressed charges and the judge had denied bail, so he wouldn't be getting out of jail for a long, long while. And the divorce would be going through in a couple of weeks.

In other words, a new world waited for her when she woke up in the morning. She'd be on her own, responsible for herself and her kids, making decisions and setting goals. Proving that she was her own person.

All of which she would have to do without the man she loved.

But that intention, she realized suddenly, made no sense. Why would she deliberately reject the chance for a fulfilling relationship? Just because he hadn't professed his undying love? She hadn't exactly laid her heart out for him, either.

So Susannah decided that her first choice, in this new life of hers, must be to take a risk and fight for her own happiness. The secure life she wanted—for her children as well as herself—could be created right here on the Circle M, with the man who showed an unquestionable commitment to those he loved.

She turned around and looked up at Wyatt. "We need to talk."

"Okay..."

She glanced around at the crowd. "Not here."

"Anywhere particular you'd like to go?"

Somewhere romantic, somewhere meaningful, somewhere she was comfortable… "The kitchen. We can take some of these empty serving plates to the house."

Strangely, none of the other adults offered to help, though Caroline did say she would watch Amber, who was dancing herself silly. As they walked down the hill, Susannah realized the rain had stopped and the sky was clearing.

"Tomorrow should be a good day," Wyatt commented.

"I hope so." The next few minutes would decide.

Once in the kitchen, she resisted the urge to start loading the dishwasher. With only the light over the sink switched on, she faced Wyatt across the breakfast counter.

"Earlier this summer, you said I needed the opportunity to make my own choices, to decide what I wanted my life to be."

"I believe everybody deserves that chance."

"But then you took away one of my options. Essentially, you made the decision for me."

He frowned. "How did I do that?"

"After we kissed the first time, you told me we couldn't get involved because I should go out on my own and determine what I wanted to do with my life. You also said you didn't want to be involved with a woman who wouldn't stay."

Leaning forward, he braced his forearms on the counter. "I did say that."

Susannah nodded. "But, in the time since, I have come to a conclusion of my own."

He raised an eyebrow in question.

"You were wrong." She clasped her hands near his, looking down at them. "I was in a bad situation, married since I was too young to a flawed man. But I'm thirty years old now, not innocent and not naïve. I know my own mind and what I want from life." After a moment, she lifted her gaze to his. "You."

After a moment of silence, he said, "You're sure of that?"

Susannah nodded. "I'm sure that I can take Nathan and Amber to Casper tomorrow, settle into our little apartment and start fresh. I'm prepared to work as hard as it takes to give my children safety and stability while they're growing up. I'll get my high school certificate and maybe a college degree, too. I'm determined to take care of them and myself. And I'll do it alone, if I have to."

She put her hands over his. "But what I really want is to share my accomplishments with you. To smile with you during the good times. To feel your arms around me when Nate leaves home for college or Amber gets her first apartment. To watch the delight on your face when our first grandchild is born. I love you, Wyatt. My choice is to make you a part of my life for as long as possible."

His hands shifted to grip hers. "Susannah—"

"You have a choice, too," she said, holding his gaze. "You don't have to decide for me, only for yourself. If you don't want me…if you don't feel the same way—" she drew a deep breath "—then I will be just fine on my own. I promise. You don't have to feel responsible."

"That's good to know." For the first time, he smiled at her. "Although I do try to be a responsible kind of man."

"Yes. That's one of the things I love about you."

Keeping her hands clasped in his, he came around the end of the counter to stand in front of her. "And some of the things I love about you are your determination and independence. I have no doubt that you can go out and achieve every goal you set for yourself and your kids. You're a strong woman."

Her cheeks flaming with embarrassment, Susannah stared up at him with hope blocking her throat.

Wyatt pulled her closer, setting his hands at her waist. "I wasn't used to making choices about my life. I expected the future and the past to look about the same. Maybe I figured I didn't deserve a choice." He shrugged a shoulder. "I hadn't considered that possibility until you came along. My barriers were pretty strong, I guess.

"But Tuesday, when I almost lost you, the wall came crashing down. I realized I could stay where I was, or I could take the risk of being happy and share my time with the woman I want more than I've ever wanted anything or anyone."

He lowered his head and kissed her with tender passion, and an immense joy swelled up in her heart. She leaned into him and circled her arms around his neck, reveling in the closeness she'd thought she would never feel again.

Long before she was ready, Wyatt drew away. "So I'm making a choice, too. I choose to offer you my home and myself, with no strings. If you want me, I'm yours."

Closing her arms around his shoulders, she gave him as strong a hug as she could manage. "Wyatt Marshall, you're a smart man—another thing I love about you. Now, kiss me again, and don't stop for a very long time."

His arms wound tight around her, and he grinned. "It will be my pleasure, ma'am."

BECKY WOKE UP early on Saturday morning and lay in bed as streaks of sunlight crept across the bedroom floor. Her feelings tilted like a teeter-totter between gladness and gloom.

Last night had been amazingly, wonderfully incredible. In front of everybody, Nate had kissed her. And then he'd danced with her the rest of the night, which pretty much made them a couple. They hadn't gotten a chance for another kiss—the grown-ups kept a pretty close watch on them after the first one. But when they'd said good-night, his smile had been all for her.

Today, though…today was the end of camp. She wouldn't be seeing Nate every day, all day. Wouldn't be riding her horse or joking with Mr. Dylan or sitting by a bonfire listening to Mr. Ford sing. By lunchtime, she'd be at home again, dealing with whatever condition her mom was in, listening to the blare of the TV competing with the roar of the radio. The usual chaos.

Then, in a few days, school would start. And Nate wouldn't be there. So she had a boyfriend she would never see. Fun times.

But when she stepped inside the bunkhouse as part of the crew to fix their last breakfast, he grabbed her by the arms and turned her around. "Guess what! Guess what's happened! They're together!"

"Who?"

"My mom and Mr. Wyatt. I was *sure* they liked each other. And they finally figured it out, too. That means I don't have to move away. I get to stay here, on the Circle M." He winked at her. "And I get to go to my regular school."

"Oh, wow." There were too many grown-ups in the room to give him a hug, so she settled for a big grin. "That's awesome!"

The good news got them both through breakfast with a smile, though they were the only ones—the rest of the kids were moping over the chore of packing their stuff to head home. Cleanup took as long as possible, but there wasn't much hope for delaying the process. Sooner or later, they would have to get in the van and drive away.

At ten o'clock, they gathered in front of the house where everything had started back in June. The Marshall brothers were standing there, along with Ms. Caroline, Ms. Susannah and Dr. Rachel. Amber sat on the steps to the porch with Honey right by her side.

Nobody had said a word, but Becky realized she was going to cry.

Then Mr. Dylan spoke up. "Your last chance to hear one of our lectures." All the kids pretended to groan, and he grinned. "Yeah, yeah. I just wanted to say that we've enjoyed working with you, even when things didn't go as planned. Each of you has taught us about patience, respect and compassion. We're grateful we got the chance to know you, to learn from you."

Mr. Garrett pushed his hat back on his head. "I admire each of you for having the spirit to come here and succeed. It takes courage to change, and you've all changed in ways you might not even recognize right now." He swallowed hard. "I will always remember you in my prayers."

Mr. Wyatt cleared his throat. "Good-byes are hard," he said. "We're going to miss having you all around, causing trouble and making us laugh. You've done a good job this summer, pitching in, taking care of yourselves and your animals. We're proud of you. And you can be proud of yourselves."

Mr. Ford stepped forward. "So when you're confronted with the chance to really mess up—and you will be, don't doubt that for a minute—try to remember this summer and everything you've achieved. Remember we'll be thinking about you, rooting for you to make the right choice. We trust you to know what that right choice is."

Becky wiped her cheeks with her fingers. Lizzie had mascara streaking her face and Lena had turned her head away. Thomas pretended to sneeze, and he wiped his sleeve over his eyes.

Marcos was frowning. "Thanks," he said suddenly. "For everything." He marched over and hugged them all, starting with Mr. Ford. He finished with a pat on the head for Amber. "*Hasta la vista, amigos.*"

Then he picked up his bag and went to sit in the van.

When everybody else had done the same thing, Mr. Ford and Ms. Caroline got into the van with them. And they all went home.

December

WYATT STOOD IN the living room, appreciating the changes in his life. He'd lived here for close to twenty Christmases but never seen the house look so incredible, so festive and homey. A nine-foot tree occupied one corner, decorated with multicolored lights and ornaments chosen by a five-year-old—elves and reindeer and Santas, angels and candy canes. Greenery and candles graced the mantle, with more candles in the windows and a cluster of mistletoe hanging over the dining room entrance. So far, he hadn't had a chance to utilize that particular trimming, much to his dismay. He'd make a point of it tonight.

Among all the other special plans he had in mind.

The crunch of truck tires on snow drew Honey to the front door. She sniffed at the threshold and then barked, in case Wyatt hadn't noticed.

"I heard," he told her, reaching for the knob. "Back up, so I can get out."

Together they stepped onto the front porch in time to see Ford rounding the hood of the van to open the passenger door for Caroline. Snow had been falling since early that morning, accumulating about two feet at this point. But Wyatt had used the tractor to clear space for parking and a path up the hill to the cabin and the barn, while Nate had shoveled a walkway across the yard. Between the snow and Susannah's outside trimmings—lights on the trees near the house, garlands around the doors and windows and a huge lighted wreath on the side of the barn—the place looked like a winter wonderland, if he did say so himself. She'd even decked the cabin, where she and Nate and Amber had been staying, with white lights, a wreath on the door and candles in the windows, making even that simple building special.

Ford opened the side door of the van and the teenagers climbed out, chattering, laughing and exclaiming as they picked their way toward the house.

Nate came outside as Thomas and Lizzie reached the porch. "Hey, man." Thomas let go of Lizzie's hand to slap Nate on the shoulder. Then he shook Wyatt's hand. "It's good to see the place. Thanks for asking us."

"You're welcome anytime. Not just for parties."

Lizzie bent down to hug Honey. "It's so beautiful with all the snow. You should have a Christmas camp."

Wyatt chuckled. "Would you get up at six in the morning in the dark to drive hay around the fields?"

She straightened and smiled at him. "Maybe not, but I would help Ms. Susannah have your breakfast ready when you came in."

"That's an important job." He opened the door and ushered them in. "You can put your coats in the guest room—first door on the hallway. Check out the dining room for food."

As Thomas and Lizzie went inside, Justino, Lena and Marcos climbed the porch steps. "It's soooo cold." Lena hugged herself in her furry coat. "I need to get in by the fireplace." She hurried inside as Wyatt continued to hold the door.

"She's been cold since September," Justino said. "One day we'll go live in California, where it's always warm."

Marcos rolled his eyes. "You'd think they were already married." He shook Wyatt's hand. "Not me, man. Too many pretty girls in this world to settle on just one." With his customary swagger, he entered the house.

Nate stepped to the edge of the porch as Becky approached with Ford and Caroline. "I wondered where you were," he told the girl, holding out his hand. "Come inside and get warm."

She didn't immediately join him but motioned for him to come down, instead. "It's so pretty out here. I want to walk in the snow. I've got my boots on."

"How about doing that after getting something to eat?" Nate said, grinning. "My mom made meatballs and I've been waiting all day to sample them."

Becky shook her head. "Boys and their food." She looked over at Caroline. "Does it ever change?"

Caroline laughed. "Not that I've noticed. Getting fed regularly is at the top of most men's lists."

"I thought so." Taking Nate's hand, Becky followed him into the house.

Ford tilted his head as he gazed at Caroline. "Food is not at the top of most men's lists. You know that, right?"

Pretending to frown, she punched him in the arm. "I wasn't going to say anything else to a thirteen-year-old."

He grinned at her. "Just so you're aware."

"You two need a honeymoon," Wyatt said, feeling his cheeks burn a little. "This is Wyoming, remember. Not Hawaii." His heart beat faster at the idea of a honeymoon. Not much longer now...

"June," Ford said. "June fifth, if I survive till then." He put an arm around Wyatt's shoulders. "Everything going okay on the ranch?"

Wyatt shifted his attention back to the moment. "Great. Nate's a big help with the feeding. Between us, the hired hands and I are keeping an eye on the mama cows. Don't see any signs of early births." Caroline went inside and Ford followed, with Wyatt and Honey bringing up the rear. "The real work will start come January."

"Count me in," Ford said as he helped Caroline remove her coat. "Even though I'm living in town, I'll take shifts whenever you need a break."

"Thanks for the offer." Just as Wyatt stepped away from the door, it opened again. Laughing, Dylan and his fiancée, Jess Granger, blew into the house.

"We had a snowball fight," Dylan explained, when he'd caught his breath. "I won."

"You did not," she said. "I knocked you down with that last throw. That means I win." Having realized she wouldn't be happy without him, the reporter had returned to Wyoming for good in November, after she'd surprised Dylan at his gallery showing in Denver.

Since then, the youngest Marshall had recovered his energy, style and enthusiasm. "My fall was unrelated to your pitch," he insisted facetiously. "I slipped. Complete coincidence."

"We believe Jess," Ford said. "You lose."

Dylan put a hand over his heart. "It's a conspiracy. My own family, ranged against me."

"You have such a hard life," Wyatt chided him. "In

the meantime, have you heard from Garrett? He went to pick up Rachel in town, and I expected them to be here by now." The most important part of the evening couldn't take place until Garrett arrived.

Jess frowned. "I hope she didn't have an emergency to deal with."

Her irrepressible fiancé waved the worry away. "They'll be here shortly. What can I get you to drink, Jess? Caroline? Come have something to eat, if the kids will let us reach the table."

Rather than trying to squeeze through the crowd, Wyatt went down the hallway to reach the kitchen, where Susannah and Amber were setting peanut-blossom cookies on a serving platter.

"Is everybody here?" Susannah asked. She looked especially beautiful tonight in a sparkling white sweater and white slacks, wearing her shining hair pinned up in a fancy twist. The diamonds he'd given her as an early Christmas present glittered like stars in her ears. "We're just finishing up." Her intimate smile shared her expectation of what tonight would mean for the two of them.

He hated being the bearer of bad news. "We're still waiting for Garrett and Rachel."

The smile vanished and her brows drew together. "Do you think something's happened?"

"Maybe a late patient at the office." He shrugged, trying for reassurance. "I doubt there's anything to worry about. The road between the ranch and town isn't hard to drive, even in two feet of snow."

"But it's not like Garrett or Rachel not to keep in touch."

"No."

"Look how pretty our cookies are," Amber commanded. "And they taste good, too."

"They do?" With a wink at her, he took the cookie she'd just put in place and popped it into his mouth. "Yum," he said as he chewed.

"These are for company," she protested. "They get first pick. And you're not supposed to talk while you chew."

"Forgive me?" He stole another treat. "They're too good to resist."

Amber put her hands on her hips. "Stop that!"

Though she was smiling, Susannah shook her head at him. "I agree. Amber, let's carry these cookies into the dining room. There's a place on the table next to the cake."

Wyatt followed and soon blended into the party. He sampled Susannah's meatballs—definitely worth waiting for—and took a plate of food with him as he migrated from group to group, listening to the various conversations. Jess, Lizzie and Thomas were talking about writing, an interest they shared, while Marcos and Dylan traded their impressions of the National Finals Rodeo which had just finished up in Las Vegas. Marcos, it seemed, was still interested in doing some bull riding of his own. In the living room, Caroline, Justino and Lena discussed the most recent movies from Hollywood. Nate and Becky sat close together on the sofa, as intent on each other as if they hadn't been together in weeks, though school had only ended the day before. Wyatt chose not to intrude.

Every so often, in each group, someone would glance at the door. They were all beginning to worry about Garrett and Rachel. His mind had been preoccupied with the celebration he'd been anticipating for weeks—months!—but now, Wyatt worried, too.

In the kitchen again, he found Ford and Susannah

with Amber, who sat at the breakfast counter working on her own plate of food. "I only took two cookies," she said as he came in. "I wanted to be sure there was enough for everybody."

"Good thinking, sweetheart." He bent to kiss the top of her head. "I bet your mom will make more if all these get eaten."

"And I'll help, like I did today." She speared a meatball with her fork and put it in her mouth. Her pink cheeks bulged with the effort to chew and swallow.

Wyatt grinned and turned to share the sight with her mother. But Susannah and Ford weren't watching. Their faces showed concern as they talked quietly together.

"Garrett and Rachel?" he asked as he joined them.

"It's almost nine thirty," Susannah said. "He left before seven."

Ford glanced at the window, which showed snow still falling. "Maybe I should go after them."

Wyatt shook his head. "Then we'd have both of you wandering around in the dark. We'll get a call from somebody, eventually. Or else—"

A commotion erupted in the living room with cries of "It's about time!"

"Looks like they're here." The three of them shared a grin of relief and Wyatt said, "Let's go rib them for being late."

Judging by their appearance, Garrett and Rachel had already endured a hard time, thanks to Mother Nature, at least. They had shed their coats out on the porch, but Garrett's shirt and jeans were wet and streaked with dirt, his boots soaked. Rachel's usually neat hair was hanging loose and damp, her jeans wet to the hip. Her knee-high suede boots might never recover.

"I'm sorry," Garrett said directly to Wyatt. "It's been

a…challenging couple of hours. We would have called, but there was no phone service. Zero bars. And we've been less than five miles away the whole time."

"As long as you're both okay, that's all we care about. What happened?"

"I didn't get out of the clinic until after seven," Rachel said. "We left my place about seven thirty, drove through town and turned onto the county highway. The road had been plowed, but the snow had built up again. All at once, a truck pulling a horse trailer came up behind us, going way too fast. Then it passed us."

Ford shook his head. "Crazy."

"With a predictable result." Garrett took over the story. "Not a minute after passing our car, the driver lost control, went into a slide and coasted sideways into the mounds of snow left by the plow on the side of the road."

Susannah brought in coffee for Rachel and for Garrett, who took a sip and grinned. "Thanks. My insides are almost as cold as it is outside. Anyway, we stopped to check if the driver was okay. She was an older woman, pretty shaken up but not hurt. There were two horses in the trailer, which were fine, as far as I could tell. But she couldn't pull her truck out of the snow—she had no chains, bad tires and too much weight in the trailer for the truck engine. We didn't have phone service to call anyone for help, and who knows if there was a tow truck in Buffalo or Casper available to come, anyway? So we spent the last two hours digging snow away from the truck and trailer to get them unstuck and on their way."

"With your hands?" Wyatt asked.

"The driver had a manure fork in the trailer," Rachel said. "It works if you don't try to pick up too much snow."

Garrett gave him a two-fingered salute off an imaginary hat brim. "And my older brother warned me always to keep a shovel in my truck during the winter, just in case. I'm glad I was smart enough to listen to him."

"We all are," Caroline said. "Now you should have something to eat. There's plenty of food left."

Garrett got to his feet. "I'm going to change first." He put a hand on Rachel's shoulder. "You could at least get out of those wet boots. And I can lend you a comb." Smiling, he fingered through her messy red hair.

As was often the case, Susannah had a better solution. "Why don't we walk up to the cabin, Rachel? I can lend you dry clothes, boots, whatever you need."

"That would be wonderful."

Lizzie and Becky volunteered to keep an eye on Amber. Once they settled on the sofa with the little girl and a book, the two women went outside with Ford as an escort. The teenagers and Dylan regrouped around the refreshments.

Garrett caught Wyatt's eye. "Ready?"

Wyatt blew out a breath. "Only since August."

"Let me get changed, then, and we'll set about making this happen."

"Right." In his own room, Wyatt changed his plaid shirt for a light blue one, put on a navy-striped tie and a dark jacket. He combed his hair and then held his own gaze in the mirror for a few moments. "I do," he said quietly.

He dawdled in the kitchen until Susannah returned to the house with Rachel and Ford. After a few minutes, Susannah joined him by the breakfast bar. With the door closed to the dining room, they were more or less alone.

"You look wonderful." She put her hands on his lapels. "Does that mean it's going to happen?"

Linking his hands behind her waist, he bent to kiss her forehead. "If that's what you want."

"So much," she whispered, raising her face to his. "I can't wait another day."

He kissed her lightly…but her lips yielded under his and the desire he'd kept banked for so long flared inside him, seeking more. Susannah's arms came around his neck and he tightened his hold, pressing her against him.

But then a loud laugh from the dining room drew Wyatt back to the present. He gentled his kisses and finally managed to pull away. "Whoa," he said, his voice rough. "Got a little bit lost there."

Susannah was blushing. "So much for my lipstick. I'm glad I brought it with me. I'll just take a couple of minutes."

"Sure." He'd waited all his life for Susannah. Another two minutes didn't matter.

As she came into the kitchen again, Garrett followed, wearing his clerical shirt and coat. He smiled when he saw them together. "You are a very handsome couple."

Wyatt glanced at Susannah, who said, "And you're going to make us official. Immediately."

"My pleasure."

In the living room, Garrett went to stand in front of the fireplace, with Wyatt and Susannah to the side. He raised a hand and his voice. "Can I get everybody's attention?"

The noise died away as the kids and grown-ups turned in their direction.

Amber scrambled off of the sofa, where she'd been sitting with Becky and Lizzie, and went to take Susannah's hand. "Is it time?" she whispered in a voice everyone could hear. "Did I keep the secret okay?"

Susannah bent to pick her up. "You did beautifully, sweetheart. Yes, you can tell them."

The little girl faced the crowd and held up her arms. "They're getting married! Right now!"

Dylan, standing by the front door with Nate, narrowed his eyes, staring at them. "Are you serious? Tonight?" he demanded. Then he grinned. "That's terrific!"

Garrett nodded. "Wyatt and Susannah have chosen to say their wedding vows with you all as witnesses."

There were gasps and exclamations. "Cool," Thomas said.

"I've never been to a wedding before," Marcos commented. "Does it count if it's not in church?"

Garrett nodded. "I'm here, so it counts."

"Does that mean I'm a bridesmaid?" Lena asked. "I always wanted to be a bridesmaid."

"Of course," Susannah said, setting Amber on her feet. "You all are my attendants." She looked down as she squeezed her daughter's hand. "And this is my maid of honor."

"Awesome," Becky and Lizzie in unison.

Garrett cleared his throat. "Now, if you'll all gather around, we'll transform this party into a wedding!"

The next few minutes passed all too quickly. Wyatt focused on Susannah, her soft, slender hand holding his, her sweet voice promising that she would be his wife, his woman, for the rest of her life. He made his own responses carefully, deliberately, empowering every word with all his heart and soul.

Then there was the kiss—he kept it short and sweet— and a cheer which shook the rafters. They turned to face the crowd and the first person in front of them was Nate, his smile wide as he hugged his mother and shook Wyatt's hand.

"Good job keeping the secret," Wyatt told him. "Even Becky was surprised."

"It's been fun," Nate replied. "Knowing something Dylan didn't."

Wyatt chuckled. "That's true."

In the next moment, Ford took hold of his shoulders. "Congratulations, Boss. You jumped in front of the rest of us."

"I'm not getting any younger," Wyatt said. "We wanted to make a start on the rest of our lives." He did like that word *our*.

Ford glanced at Caroline, who was giving Susannah a hug. "I empathize. Believe me. In the meantime—" he gave Wyatt a clap on the back "—I believe I should welcome my new sister to the family. Susannah, let me kiss the bride!"

The party lasted for another couple of hours as they all shared cake and sparkling cider and happiness. There was even some impromptu dancing in the living room, because the kids needed to work off the sugar they'd been eating. Garrett and Rachel demonstrated the salsa they'd been practicing, applauded by Lena and Justino, and then Ford and Caroline shared the floor with Dylan and Jess for a two-step.

"I never learned to dance," Wyatt confessed to Susannah as they stood watching. "You still have a chance for an annulment."

"You're not getting away so easy," she told him. "I never tried Western dancing, either. We'll learn together."

"It's a date."

Finally, when Wyatt was beginning to think he'd be sharing his wedding night with the whole crowd, the teenagers figured out it was time to go home. Ford and

Caroline made no effort to persuade them differently but got them into their coats and out into the snow with reasonable efficiency.

"Congratulations," Thomas said, shaking Wyatt's hand. "Can we come back again?"

"You're always welcome," Wyatt assured him. "We'll have a reunion trail ride when it warms up."

"Excellent," the boy said with a thumbs-up sign. Then he took Lizzie's hand and led her to the van.

"It was a beautiful wedding," Lena told Susannah as she and Justino left. "I hope ours is as nice one day."

As the couple left, Susannah laughed with Wyatt. "That's called planning ahead, I guess."

Nate came onto the porch from seeing Becky to the van. "Man, I wish I could drive," he said as he went into the house.

"Two years till he gets his learner's permit," Wyatt whispered to Susannah. "Then you're in for some fun."

"You're the one with experience," she replied. "I thought I'd let you handle the driving chores." She winked at him. "There's still time for an annulment."

He opened the screen door for her. "Not a chance. Even if it means teaching teenagers to drive."

Garrett, Rachel, Dylan and Jess had somehow managed to put away the leftover food and straighten the kitchen while they'd been outside saying good-bye.

"I'm planning to cook Sunday lunch for everybody," Susannah told them as they left. "Pot roast."

Rachel and Garrett looked at each other and burst out laughing. "Private joke," she explained. "I'll see you then."

Dylan and Jess waved as they walked off in the snow, heading toward Dylan's barn. "See you tomorrow, Boss. Don't worry about chores. I've got things under control."

"Thanks." With relief, Wyatt shut the front door and found Susannah standing inside with a sleepy Amber on her hip. "Just us," she said. "At last."

"At last." He noticed where she was standing—in the doorway to the dining room, directly underneath the mistletoe—and went to join her. "I've been waiting for this moment all day long.

"First, you." He bent close and kissed Amber on the cheek. She gave a drowsy smile.

Then he put a hand under Susannah's chin. "And now, Mrs. Marshall—"

Nate barged through the door from the kitchen, a cookie in each hand. "Oh, geez. Are you guys going to be making out all over the place?"

"Of course not," Susannah said, her cheeks turning bright pink.

"Get over here," Wyatt instructed. "It's an important moment." When the boy came to stand beside him, Wyatt put a hand on his shoulder. "Welcome to the Marshall family, all three of you. Thanks for joining us."

"'And God bless us, every one,'" Nate quoted, in a Tiny Tim voice.

"Damn right," Wyatt said and, ignoring the teenager's pained expression, leaned over to give his wife a mistletoe kiss. "God bless us, every one!"

* * * * *

SPECIAL EXCERPT FROM

H HARLEQUIN®
™

Western Romance

Will Laredo and Cassidy McCullough have been at odds
since they were kids, until they rescue a baby and find
themselves fighting attraction instead of each other.

Read on for a sneak preview of
THE RANCHER AND THE BABY,
the next book in USA TODAY *bestselling author*
Marie Ferrarella's ***FOREVER, TEXAS*** *miniseries.*

She raised her eyes again, expecting to meet his, but Will
was once again strictly focused on the road ahead. She felt
something almost weird for a second.

"Are we having a moment here?" she asked him.

Will wasn't able to read her tone of voice and decided
that the wisest thing was just to acknowledge her words in
the most general possible sense.

"I suppose that some people might see it that way," he
said.

Cassidy shook her head. "Typical."

"Come again?"

Cassidy raised her voice. "I said your answer's typical.
You're a man who has never committed to anything."

"Not true." Will contradicted her before he could think
better of it.

"Okay, name one thing," she challenged.

She was not going to box him in if that was what
she was looking to do, he thought. At least, not about
something that was way too personal to talk about out
loud with her. Besides, he did just fine having everyone

think that he was only serious about any relationship he had for a very limited amount of time. That way, if he brought about the end himself, he never had to publicly entertain the sting of failure.

"I'm committed to restoring my father's ranch, making it into the paying enterprise it should have been and still could be with enough effort," he told her.

"You mean that?"

Rather than say yes, he told her, "I never say something just to hear myself talk."

"There's some difference of opinion on that one, but—"

"Look," he began, about to tell her that he didn't want to get into yet another dispute with her over what amounted to nothing, but he never had the opportunity. The one thing that Cassidy admittedly could do better than anyone he knew was outtalk everyone.

"—if you're really serious about that," she was saying, "I can probably manage to help you out a few hours on the weekends." The way she saw it, she did owe it to him for helping her save the baby, and she hated owing anyone, most of all him.

Will spared her a glance before he went back to watching the road intently. Cassidy had managed to do the impossible.

She had rendered him completely speechless.

Don't miss
THE RANCHER AND THE BABY
by Marie Ferrarella, available December 2016
wherever Harlequin® Western Romance®
books and ebooks are sold.

www.Harlequin.com

HWREXP1116

HARLEQUIN®

A *Romance* FOR EVERY MOOD™

Love the Harlequin book you just read?

Your opinion matters.

Review this book on your favorite book site, review site, blog or your own social media properties and share your opinion with other readers!

HARLEQUIN®

A Romance FOR EVERY MOOD™

Stay up-to-date on all your
romance-reading news with the
Harlequin Shopping Guide,
**featuring bestselling authors, exciting new
miniseries, books to watch and more!**

The newest issue will be delivered right to you
with our compliments! There are 4 each year.

Signing up is easy.

EMAIL

ShoppingGuide@Harlequin.ca

WRITE TO US

HARLEQUIN BOOKS
Attention: Customer Service Department
P.O. Box 9057, Buffalo, NY 14269-9057

OR PHONE

1-800-873-8635 in the United States
1-888-343-9777 in Canada

Please allow 4-6 weeks for delivery of the first issue by mail.